FIGHT THE PEACE

FIGHT THE PEACE

THE HEINOUS CRIMES OF SARA SLICK™ BOOK 3

ST BRANTON   CM RAYMOND   LE BARBANT

LMBPN Publishing
PMB 196, 2540 South Maryland Pkwy
Las Vegas, NV 89109

First US edition, June, 2020
ebook ISBN: 978-1-64971-018-5
Print ISBN: 978-1-64971-019-2

THE FIGHT THE PEACE TEAM

Thanks to our Beta Readers
Larry Omans, Kelly O'Donnell, Rachel Beckford, Allen Collins

Thanks to our JIT Readers

Kerry Mortimer
Jeff Goode
Deb Mader
Paul Westman

Editor

SkyHunter Editing Team

PROLOGUE

Breathe in. Breathe out. Breathe in. Breathe out.

It was all she could do. When she stopped focusing on the breaths filling her lungs and sliding out again, the panic crept up along her spine and stung in the hairs on the back of her neck. But with every breath, the cell felt smaller. It closed in around her, the slimy, cold walls creeping in. It had been the same way for the last several days since she got tossed in there.

She didn't know why she was there. She didn't know what was going on. The only thing she could concentrate on was keeping it together. So far, she'd been able to do it. She wasn't screaming or gnashing her teeth. She hadn't started crawling up the walls or trying to wedge herself between the narrow bars. But it was getting close.

The door to the cell opened, and her kidnapper walked in. Having its presence in the same space made her stomach turn, but she refused to show fear. She wouldn't give it that satisfaction. She couldn't see its face in the dark, but could feel the evil that radiated off it.

"Whatever you want from me, you won't get it," she said, her voice tough.

It laughed and stepped closer. "I already have it," the stranger sneered.

It ducked and put its face close to hers. Even in the faint light, she could see it more clearly. She gasped and scrambled back across the cold floor, recoiling from what she saw.

Her face stared back at her.

CHAPTER ONE

Sara Slick, master of espionage.

That would be on my freaking tombstone if I wasn't careful. I pushed aside the door of the closet that had been my hiding place for the last thirty minutes, then poked my head out and checked for any traces of the voices I heard only a few moments before. Thankfully, the room appeared empty, and the door locked shut, so I slipped out and into the darkness.

The boat rocked and my stomach felt like it might involuntarily remove my lunch for me, but I forced it back down. Getting used to it shouldn't have been so bad since it was a giant freighter ship and was docked at that. But perhaps shrimp tacos, ice cream, French fries, and at least two liters of soda weren't the best choice for a light lunch pre-game.

A hot burp bubbled up, and I tried to keep my belch from being too loud and alerting the people I was hiding from. I shoved my face inside my jacket, let it loose, and immediately felt a furious Splinter wriggling in my pocket.

How he had the gall to be upset at anyone else's smell defied logic, but I patted the side of my jacket to soothe him anyway.

"Sorry, buddy," I muttered, and took in my surroundings.

The room was on a lower deck of the ship and wasn't where I had planned on being. I had thrown myself in there in an attempt to avoid being caught by one of the most foul-smelling Farsiders I had come across since leaving The Deep. My grappling hook was still attached at the top of the anchor, and now I faced the possibility of someone noticing that to the rest of the risk of the mission. The revelers stumbling around in the lights and glamor of Atlantic City might take selfies and post about it on whatever stupid app I was still three lessons behind on. Apparently, this was where they stored food carts when they weren't in use, and the sailor who nearly caught me was either too hungover or too stupid to notice me diving behind one when he came in to grab a silver tray.

Either way, they stayed for a while, chit-chatting in a language that sounded like something out of an old James Bond movie. My legs felt like they were steel rods before I got out. Then one of them came back, and I hid in the closet. Now I stood in the empty room, surrounded by empty carts and looking for a trace of evidence that would show we were right in suspecting this particular freighter.

"What was that?" came the voice on the headset I wore. It was Archie, and his slightly confused tone told me he thought I'd meant my apology to Splinter for him.

"Nothing. I was talking to my rat." I inched closer to the door. I couldn't hear anything going on outside it, but that meant nothing. I needed to crack it open to make sure the room wasn't soundproof.

"It's fine, Slick," came Ally's voice. She was undoubtedly still standing above the table with the blueprints of the ship laid out before her. She was so damned excited to roll them out. I didn't have the heart to tell her I had memorized most of it over the last few days. Having her in my ear with her eyes on the prints meant I had a backup. "Did you see anyone? Could you tell what they were?"

"Nah," I responded. "Too busy not getting caught. I'll let you know if I figure them out."

I had been invisible so far. I planned on remaining invisible for as long as possible. Hopefully, the shimmying up the side of a ship only a few miles from the Boardwalk in Atlantic City in broad daylight wasn't enough of a spectacle for anyone to notice. I figured most people were too busy getting hammered, looking at their phone, or desperately trying to figure out how to explain little Bobby's college money suddenly being the property of a casino to look too closely to a dank-looking cargo ship. So far, no one had sounded an alarm, so I'd take that as a win for me, loss for society kind of situation.

The Farsiders on today's menu were a motley crew, picked from all over The Far. While staking out the ship since it docked, I saw a couple of trolls, a creature who looked like a hedgehog on a tremendous amount of steroids and with a dentist bent on making sure it could eat even the toughest meat, and a few fairies. The fairies I was prepared for.

They weren't the cute little winged creatures I plastered posters of on my wall when I was nine. These were long, lithe, and absolutely evil things with sharp teeth and a penchant for tricking humans into terrible situations. Run-ins with fairies usually weren't fun, and they could be fast and strong. Having one shadowed by a troll would be the worst kind of logistical nightmare.

Which was exactly what was happening right then.

I looked out the tiny window on the door and saw a short, squat, grey mass standing by another door a little way down and on the other side of the hallway. A fairy stood by it, speaking to it, then went inside the room. I could only guess that was where they kept some of the lizard people since it was guarded. If it wasn't, there were likely some secrets in there, and that was enticing on its own. I looked on the other side and saw two more trolls blocking the hallway, standing side by side. They were looking in another direction, which made things much easier.

"Ok, guys. Looks like I have three trolls and a room with at least one fairy in it. Two are south, blocking the hall, and one is north in the room across from me. See it, Ally?" I asked.

"I do. That's the place."

"Slick, it's Archie," Archie informed me. He never failed to do that, no matter how many times Ally patiently explained there were only two people it could be, and she didn't sound like a middle-aged man doing a bad George Bush Jr. impression. Not that she hadn't tried.

"Yeah, Archie. I hear you," I muttered.

"Slick, a friendly reminder that the lizards may not be very receptive to your help at first. You need to be careful with them. They are hearty creatures, but they can get rather jumpy," he cautioned.

"Funny." I swept my eyes over the hallway and noticed the trolls not only didn't move, they didn't seem to breathe. They looked like they reverted to being giant rocks when standing still. It hurt my eyes to look at them and continue to make out their features when they weren't moving around. "I was always told lizard people secretly ran the world. At least, it's what the tinfoil-hat guy said on public access at three AM."

"Oh, God, no. No one would let them run anything. Not even humans. They're gross," he stated matter-of-factly.

I laughed heavily at Archie using gross to describe anything, then realized that whatever it was he thought was gross, I would be in direct contact with it in a matter of minutes. Assuming I could get through the wall of walking gravel that was the three trolls.

"One other thing," Archie interjected. "Remember, the Lights Out rune is a last resort. I know I told you before…"

"Multiple times," I muttered under my breath.

"But it bears repeating. I'm not entirely sure it will work. I'm also not entirely sure it won't cause a mild nuclear explosion. So be aware," he warned.

"Good pep talk, Archie. I'll try not to cause a mass extinction event if possible." I patted the small, twirly, possibly nuclear catastrophe in my jacket.

It looked like a normal revolver but contained a dragon's tooth and happened to be a rune Archie hyped for days as the most powerful he'd ever created. We hadn't had a chance to test it, so neither one of us was precisely sure what it would do in action. He assured me that the risk of it exploding into a million pieces and killing me and everything else within a mile radius was around twenty percent. Tops.

I pulled out a new rune from my back pocket and cracked the door ever so slightly. It felt light in my hand, but that was deceptive. The boomerang-shaped weapon was small enough to fit into my back pocket, but a flick of the wrist could open up blades on either end. Archie called it the "Blood Seeker," which was such a suitably badass name that it instantly made me want to figure out what it could do.

Apparently, the magic imbued in it allowed it to home in on major arteries if thrown correctly, and if the blades were open, it would find and sever them, then return to me safely. It also contained a chamber that I could fill with various liquids for a more biological attack, which seemed like it might suit my current need. I pulled my arm back to throw it in an instant as I peered through the crack of the door.

Thankfully, it opened in the guard troll's direction, and I could push it open enough to aim the blade. My usual switchblade stayed safely in my other pocket, ready for me to use it when I inevitably broke or lost the boomerang. Or, more likely, figured out its catastrophic and unforeseen flaw and needed the backup of a familiar tool.

With a flick of my wrist, I sent it soaring, my thumb rubbing over the compartment switch inside at the last second. Doing so activated the poison gas compartment Archie had modified it with. The gas would release in a potent puff of air upon impact and as it hit the troll dead-on in the face, I saw the air around his head turn purple, then green, then normal again.

The boomerang effect seemed to fail almost instantly. It clattered on the floor and the troll looked over at it. He seemed to stare at it for a long time, as if the thoughts running through his mind had glacial speed and the confusion of getting hit with a U-shaped blade with a glowing rock in the middle was too difficult to work out. Then, like a balloon deflating, he sank into the wall behind him and stopped breathing.

"Poison worked, Archie," I whispered into the headset.

"Oh, thank goodness. I was almost positive it would release a hallucinogenic instead," he murmured back.

I nodded. Of course. Exactly what I would have needed, a troll on LSD. Maybe I would stick with the good old switchblade for now.

"Might need to work on the boomerang effect though," I added. "Anyway, I'm going in." I slipped out of the door at my announcement, my eyes on the two trolls guarding the hall.

CHAPTER TWO

While sneaking up to the dead troll, I noticed how awful he smelled. Not that it was a surprise a troll smelled bad—my run-ins with them were always nausea-inducing—but this time was a little different. This troll seemed to use his odor as a defense mechanism of its own. I was already having trouble keeping down my now-critical mistake of a lunch and coming into contact with a smell that warranted hazmat suits and air purifiers wasn't helping one damned bit.

I snuck a peek back at the trolls guarding the hall and noticed they weren't moving yet. Either they hadn't heard the clanging of the Blood Seeker or they didn't care. I wasn't going to ask them why. The door of the room I saw the Fae enter was heavy and cold steel, and the knob on the front looked crafted from gold. It took a minute to realize why: no one could enchant gold. If they locked the door with a traditional key, only another key or picking the lock would work. Magic had no effect. The only option at my disposal was if they left the door unlocked.

They couldn't be that stupid.

I looked back at the dead troll and the two others who stood guard facing the opposite direction.

Well, maybe.

After grabbing the Blood Seeker and putting it back in my pocket, I placed my hand on the doorknob and closed my eyes. I squeezed and tried to turn the handle, but it wouldn't budge. I gave it a little more force, but still nothing. That left only one other option, a localized explosive device Archie had put together.

It worked like a miniature C4, and he had shown it working on a door before. A small puff of smoke, an almost imperceptible sound, and it would blow up the lock on the inside, the explosion itself contained in the box attached.

I pulled the small magnetic box out of one of the many homemade pockets I had sewn into my jacket and positioned it directly over the lock mechanism. I activated the timer, looked back at the other trolls standing guard, and drew a deep breath. Just like before, a puff of smoke and a small thud accompanied the box moving ever so slightly.

Considering that unhooking the box from the lock might cause it to fall apart, I decided to press my luck and see if I could grab it on the way out. I pushed a little and the door opened, revealing a blinding white light in the room. I grinned and opened it wide. Huge mistake.

Arrows immediately shot at me, and I ducked and rolled along one wall of the room. The door shut behind me as I kept rolling while feeling the zip of the arrows flying around me and barely missing me. I finally found myself behind a table and reached up to push it over, so it acted as a barrier between the archers and me. As soon as it hit the ground, I heard the 'thwap' sound of a dozen arrows bury into it.

"Found 'em," I told Archie through my headset and grabbed the Blood Seeker. I flung it around the table, hoping its perfect balance and precision would at least take out some of the projectiles coming my way. I reached my hand on the other side of the table to wait for its return, hopefully with little streaks of blood on it.

It didn't.

"Uhh…" I muttered while waiting for the blade to return and noting it most certainly wasn't. Sound in the room seemed to disappear, and I peeked my head up over the table to look. I couldn't believe what I saw.

A collection of small, green, scaly creatures sat in the center of the room, their yellow eyes focused on one of the fairies. Two fairies lay on the floor with bright pink blood flowing from their bodies. The third Fae was nailed to the wall, the boomerang buried deep in her neck and pinning her to the plaster, her hands still on the bow and arrow she recently tried to stop my heart with.

As if on a cue, the reptilians all turned their heads toward me. Tentatively, I raised my hand and gave them a little wave.

"Hey, I'm here to rescue you. Name's Sara Slick," I introduced myself.

There was a moment of temporary silence as the reptilian creatures blinked at me. Then…pandemonium.

High-pitched screaming and chaos filled the room as the reptilians realized the person who claimed to be saving them was the infamous Sara Slick. Perhaps rehabilitating my name one rescue at a time wasn't the most effective means of self-promotion. I tried to shush them but realized pretty quickly I would have to let them scream it out. Hopefully, no new fairies were on their way, and the trolls remained exactly as dumb as I hoped they were.

"Everybody shut the hell up," I yelled and threw my hands in the air to get their attention. The room went silent as they stared at me, their weird little lizard mouths open.

"I didn't say anything," Archie hissed. There was a few seconds' pause. "It's Archie."

"She wasn't talking to you. She was talking to the screaming lizard people," Ally corrected him.

"Oh, yeah, that makes sense. An awful racket in there. I hope no one else heard," he muttered.

"Me too," Ally responded. "Could attract all sorts of bad guys."

"For the love of all that is holy…" I grumbled, then turned my attention back to the lizard people and cleared my throat. "I need everyone to chill! I'm trying to get you out of here, but I need you to be quiet and helpful, please! Thank you."

A cascade of reptilian eyes blinked at me as I held my hands in the air, waiting for them to stop moving.

"Ok, good. That's good. Now, give me one second."

I walked to the Fae impaled on the wall and removed the boomerang. When the body fell to the floor, there was an audible gasp from the lizards. I couldn't help but smirk. Fear of what I could do might be helpful. Might keep them docile enough I could escape with them. Now all I had to do was get them past the two trolls and into the elevator.

At least, I hoped the elevator could fit all of them. There were about twenty, but they were small, so, hey, this could work out. I turned around, my grin getting bigger as I tried out the lines in my head of what to say to get them to follow me.

Suddenly, as if the boat had finally undocked, it shifted. A loud horn filled the air around us. The lights flickered.

More pandemonium.

After a few minutes of corralling the ugly things and trying to explain to Ally and Archie what had happened, I stood at the door again. The room was quiet once more, and I drew a deep breath. As long as I opened the door and the trolls were still standing in the hallway, or even better, had left, I was good. I turned the knob and pulled.

Instead of an empty wall in front of me, my eyes went directly into those of a new, larger, and angry-looking troll. He stood, his jaw open and his arm reaching for the knob which I had pulled away from him. Behind him stood a new creature. I slammed the door and put my back to it.

"Uhh… Archie. What's seven feet tall, has glowing red eyes, and carries a scythe?" I asked hurriedly.

"Slick, its Archie. I don't think now is the time for riddles," he chastised.

"It's not a fucking riddle!" I exclaimed as the door behind me thunked. The troll would break through any second, and my tiny-ass body wouldn't be enough to hold them out. I had to think quick. "It's a…a…a *thing*. Outside the door. Presently trying to kill me."

"Oh, well, that's not good," he commented.

"No shit, Archie."

"Well, it could be a demon. Might be a Moloch. Did it have big horns and a snout?"

"I didn't pay that close attention, Archie. I think it might be time for Lights Out."

"Is there any other choice?" His voice sounded both resigned and excited.

The problem with Archie was sometimes his stuff worked and sometimes it didn't, but regardless, he was always so excited about it. If it weren't for the fact I was almost always the guinea pig, it wouldn't be so bad.

"Doubt it," I told him and rolled forward, then reached inside my jacket for the gun.

The rune inside glowed a dull yellow when I pulled it out and aimed at the door as the troll knocked it down. Lizard people scrambled for cover and three trolls, a Fae, and yes, a horned, snouted, red-eyed, seven-foot Moloch came in.

I aimed the gun at the Moloch and tried to prepare myself for whatever reaction it would have.

"Any last advice on a Moloch, Archie?" I yelled as my finger squeezed the trigger.

"Run," he suggested.

Nah.

I pulled the trigger, expecting a blast or a boom or even a fizzle as absolutely nothing happened. What I didn't expect was for all the sound in the room to seem like it was sucked into the barrel of the gun, then get blasted back out at ten times the volume and for all the lights to go out. In fact, all the electronics went dead.

Including my headset.

"Ah, shit."

CHAPTER THREE

Rather than worry about why all the lights went out, I decided to go ahead and swing for the fences. Or rather, toss the gun at the two glowing red eyes about ten feet in front of me. I aimed directly in between them, then tossed, ducked, and rolled to the side. There was a squishy thud and the glowing eyes jerked back, then the form collapsed to the ground as I found my feet again.

The pandemonium returned in earnest again, and bodies bumped into bodies everywhere. A sound like a roar rose from one side of the room and I felt a craggy, hard surface brush by me. Thinking fast, I went for the one weakness I knew of on trolls. I spun to gain momentum, then flung my heel into where I thought the stomach would be. The area where a belly button would be on a human was the only soft spot on a troll, and the sound that escaped the thing at the end of my foot let me know I connected with it.

One down, two to go. I rolled toward the glowing eyes, which were on the ground staring up. I patted around on the ground for the gun. When I didn't find it, I reached back to pull out my trusty switchblade. As soon as I got my fingers around it, I felt long, strong fingers close around my wrist, and in a beat, I was airborne until I crashed into a wall and slid down. The Moloch was up. I struggled to my feet as fast as I could and dove to one side, knocking over a screaming lizard person in the process.

As I got out of the way, the Moloch crashed into the wall where I had been and knocked a hole in it. When he did, light seeped into the room, and I realized we were near a deck. Something was finally going right.

"Ally, can you hear me? I'm going to the deck," I yelled into my useless headset. I figured maybe they could hear me even if I couldn't hear them. I ran for the hole in the wall and was only a few feet away when suddenly something smashed into my side and the world turned upside down as I spun in revolutions.

I crashed into a wooden chair, which exploded into pieces and sent splinters everywhere.

Splinters.

Where the hell was Splinter?

Before I could backtrack to the last time I had seen him, I had to roll to avoid a giant troll fist that crashed into the ground, for sure aiming to splatter my brains into goo. I rolled backward over my shoulder to get to my feet and dove forward at the small line of light the outside poured onto the advancing troll. It illuminated where the stomach was and I drop-kicked it hard. The troll went to one knee, and I pulled out the switchblade, then drove it deep into the back of its neck before yanking it back out. The troll went to the ground and out of sight in the darkness.

I turned my attention to the hole in the wall where I could see the Moloch in the distance, blocked by the exiting lizards as they tried to make a madcap escape for the outside. It was attempting to grab them as they ran and throw them back into the room or at other trolls as they scattered. I didn't blame them. Staying here with dead Fae and dead or dying trolls wasn't my idea of a good time either. The light shining on my face then went dark as a shadow passed in front of me. It was large, looming, and smelled of baked dogshit.

One of the trolls guarding the hallway earlier was in front of me, and it was looking for a fight.

It roared and I ducked, then rolled between its legs and made for the outside. While an angry troll was a troll prone to making mistakes in a fight, I certainly didn't want to fight one in the dark. If he wanted to come outside in the light where I could see him, I would happily kick his ass like his friend's. For now, though, my focus was on the lizard people's safety and getting the hell off the boat that was now going God knows where.

When I reached the outside, the Moloch was waiting for me. The scythe it carried buried into the wall beside me as I dodged its attack. I used the opportunity to lay some punches into its ribs and it backed up, releasing the scythe and trying to create space. I rolled toward the beast, slicing up with the switchblade and cutting it along the chest.

Obviously, a stab alone wouldn't do much, but perhaps I could weaken it. It backed up and found itself on the railing at the edge of the ship, and I saw my shot. I ran at it and leapt with both feet out, aimed at its chest. They landed perfectly, but he was too strong. I would need something other than momentum and brute force to beat this thing. Thankfully, I had prepared.

I pulled a small item from my pocket, hanging from a chain. It looked like a rather pretty necklace with a glittering silver stone in the center. The main thing separating this from something I would have bought from *Forever 21* when I was fifteen was that this one modified the force of gravity around it, meaning that when spun then thrown, whatever it hit, it hit with twenty times the force that it should. I spun the chain above my head a few times to gain the momentum it needed and hoped the thin strand of gold was enough to hold the rune before snapping and sending the powerful blast meekly off into the distance, or worse, right back in my face.

It didn't. I let it go, and it sailed through the air toward the Moloch and landed square in his chest. There was a sound like the entire world taking a deep breath, then a tiny, localized sonic boom emanated from where he stood. A surprised grunt followed the Moloch's body as it fell overboard and into the water. A colossal splash followed a moment later. I turned to look for the lizards and saw them collecting together. The trolls were nowhere in sight, and no more Fae showed up. Maybe they'd had enough? I wasn't going to question it.

"All right, guys, so I want you to remember, right? Sara Slick saved your asses. Got it? *Sara. Slick,*" I emphasized, making sure they heard me.

Feeling accomplished, I put my hands on my hips and watched as each of the lizards went from staring at me to something behind me. Then back at me. Then pandemonium again. Yes. There was a shit-ton of pandemonium.

Only this time, the pandemonium led to them hopping over the edge of the boat and into the water.

"Yeah, well, you're ugly," I shouted down at the last one as it splashed into the water. Rehabilitating my image would be harder than I thought. I turned around, fully expecting to see something menacing, but saw nothing but an empty boat. Then I heard a huge splash, and I peered over the edge. A troll was doing what it could to stay afloat and failing miserably.

But I didn't knock him into the water. He must have jumped. But why would a troll jump into the water?

I ran for the side of the boat and almost headlong into a Fae. His wild eyes were enough to tell me that one of us would move out of the narrow space for the other, and he didn't plan on it being him. I kicked forward and backed out of the way barely in time. His fists tried to make contact, but I ducked one and caught the other in the crook of my arm, then slammed my head forward into his jaw and heard a satisfying crack as it landed.

The Fae tried to back up, but I was holding him steady with his arm inside mine, and I drove my elbow into his stomach. I grabbed him by the throat and shoved him into the side of the ship.

"How many do you have aboard?" I shouted into his terrified and angry face. Spittle fell from his lips as he grasped my hand, but I had no intention of letting go. I pulled the switchblade from my pocket and held it to his chest. "How many lizards do you have on this boat?"

"Fourteen. That's all. The rest is Far weapons. Let me go!" he demanded.

Fourteen seemed roughly the amount I had found and

watched jump overboard at the sound of my name.

"That's all? Fourteen?"

"Let me go, Slick!" he insisted.

"Slick!" came another voice. This one didn't come from a Fae or a demon or a troll. It came from Ally. And it came from my headset.

I tossed the Fae off the wall and watched as he took a running leap and dove overboard, like the others. What the hell was going on?

"Ally? What's going on?"

"Slick, get out of there," she yelled.

"Slick, it's Archie," he began.

"I swear, Archie, stop introducing yourself," I snapped.

"No time, Slick," interrupted Ally. Something in her voice made me worry.

The sound of all the electronics on the boat suddenly jumping to life surrounded me and I spun around. A clicking sound from behind me caught my attention, and I looked for it. It was Splinter. He was running for me, carrying the Lights Out in his teeth. I patted my jacket and realized I had thrown at the Moloch and couldn't find it in the dark. I took it from him, and he jumped into my jacket while squeaking loudly. Something was upsetting him.

"No time for what?" I asked.

"The boat, Slick. It's heading straight for the Steel Pier!" she exclaimed.

My eyes grew wide, and I ran around the rest of the boat. When I got to the front, I saw she was right. We were heading right for the glitz and glam of the East Coast's Sin City, and fast. No wonder everyone was making a dive for it.

CHAPTER FOUR

"Where are the controls?" I shouted into the headset.

"Slick, it's a-around the corner," Archie replied, and despite everything, I was proud of him.

"Which corner?" I asked.

"The far one from where you came out. Exact opposite side. You'll have to go around rather than through," he instructed.

I took off running for the place he was talking about. I thought I knew where it was, and considering I ran to the front of the boat, it seemed like I should, theoretically, be closer to where the main controls were. Of course, I had no real frame of reference other than boat rides at theme parks, where the captain always stood at a window somewhere near the middle-front and waved at people. Part of me wondered if there was a big wooden wheel thing and if I could spin it.

Of course, if there wasn't, I had no idea how I would steer the boat away from the Steel Pier or its famous Ferris wheel. Maybe I would smash buttons until something happened. I was still planning strategy for emergency boat driving when I rounded the corner and came face-to-face with two more Fae.

"Son of a bitch," one of them gasped. "It's Sara Slick!"

Rather than engage in a lengthy conversation where I introduced myself, we got to know each other, and eventually they tried to kill me, I skipped to the end and punched the talky one in the mouth. He flew backward and skidded to a stop at the edge of the boat while I spun to round-house kick the other.

Unfortunately, this Fae was quicker on the reflexes and saw my kick coming, and ducked low to make me miss. She swept my planted leg, and I sprawled on the deck. She dove on top of me and landed a shot to my jaw that made my vision go black and stars temporarily show up while I put up my arms to block another. Her second shot was to my stomach, and I felt the air rush out of me in one motion. I was getting my ass kicked and needed to create some space. Thankfully, a space-maker was in my pocket, ready to go.

Splinter jumped out of the jacket and attacked the face of the Fae woman on top of me. She had mounted me to deliver her punches, but now she was on her back and flailing at her face as Splinter ran around biting any soft fleshy bit he could find. Figuring he had things worked out for a minute, I turned my attention to the other Fae.

He was on his knees and trying to get to his feet, but having trouble with his balance. Fae weren't known for being seafaring creatures, preferring to stick to areas with lots of trees. This suited me since my stomach finally settled and grew accustomed to the motion of the boat.

Now it was all a matter of keeping my balance due to the intense rocking and kicking his ass before we crashed and died on the Boardwalk.

I ran forward and dove while driving my knee into the side of his head, and he fell back again. I scrambled to him and grabbed him by the front of his shirt. Behind me the Fae woman was still screaming, and happy little gnawing sounds came from Splinter as he ran around her, biting constantly, and let her hit herself as she tried to catch him or hit him.

I drove my fist into the Fae's face a few times until I was reasonably sure he was unconscious, then stood. As I did, the boat rocked again, and I grabbed the railing. The Fae wasn't as lucky. His body slid toward the edge, missed the railing with his tall, thin elf frame, and slid right off the edge of the boat. His splash was accompanied a second later by one from the Fae woman, who apparently was tired of trying to hit Splinter and might have realized if she didn't save the Fae man, he would drown.

I shrugged and looked for my little buddy. He galloped up and jumped, and found his way into my jacket before ducking, then popping his head back up to beam at me. I scratched his head as I took off running for the controls. After this was all over, if I avoided destroying the Boardwalk, I owed this little guy more shrimp tacos.

When I reached a door marked Mechanical, I realized I was now on the opposite side of the boat from where I broke out. I wracked my brain for the memory of the inside schematics, but couldn't recall where the outside entrance to a mechanical closet was, so I had to ask my backup. It was going to make her life.

"Ally, I'm standing outside a door with Mechanical written over the top. How close am I to the controls?"

A small squeal on the other end was high enough I was sure Dog could hear it wherever he was. I pulled the set away from my ear for a second and shook my head. When I replaced it, Archie was sighing.

"Please, Ally, don't do that again," he implored.

"Sorry. The mechanical entrance on the outside is two doors down from the entrance to the main hold that will get you to the control room. Keep going."

I followed her instructions and found the second room and was delighted to find out it was unlocked. I yanked it open, fully expecting more trolls or Fae, but the hold was empty. Not a sound came from the area, which somehow was worse than it being full. It was abandoned. By everyone.

"I think I found the control room," I advised them as I reached a door leading into a large metal area inside the hold. I tried the door and found it locked. "I think I might need a secondary way in."

"Well," Archie began. "I was afraid of that. Do you see a keyhole?"

"No." Unlike the door where the lizard people were held, this one had a long bar on the door that wouldn't budge.

"Then it's likely magnetic. Which means it runs on electricity. Which means..." His voice trailed off.

"Lights Out." I sighed.

"Yup. Once you get in there, look for a manual way to steer the boat. There should be, in case of power failure. You need to find it and steer away from the pier."

"Got it," I confirmed, then pulled out the revolver and pointed it at the door. Part of me hoped a direct hit would only disable the one door, but as I pulled the trigger, the now-familiar sound of all electronics shutting off filled my ears. I yanked on the door, and it opened easily now. I ran inside and up the steps to the top of the control room.

I reached the top and looked around. Large windows showed a 360-degree angle of the world around me, and I rushed to the giant board of controls. I scanned them for anything I could recognize when I came across a comically small wheel. It was like the ones on every schoolyard playhouse ever, but only a foot high and made of an ornate wood.

"Worth a shot," I muttered to myself and grabbed the handles.

They were surprisingly stiff, and I pulled hard to the left. To my amazement, I felt the boat turn in that direction. I kept pulling while laughing like a madman, visions of being a pirate captain in my head as I yanked the boat away from the pier where hundreds of people ran for their lives.

I yanked with all my might and pulled on the wheel until the boat lurched and tossed me into the control board itself. An impossible sense of gravity took over, and it felt like the entire world tipped to the right. I landed on the doorframe and banged my elbow hard enough that despite the emergency, I spat out a curse. Papers and wires and folders full of instructions that would have come in handy a few minutes ago cascaded down and bounced off me and everything else nearby.

The captain's chair bolted to the floor spun helplessly,

then faced away as gravity pulled the heaviest parts toward where I lay. The boat had crashed and landed on its side, but thankfully it was at rest on the sand, avoiding the Boardwalk. That meant it was still somewhat in the water, and the sand below it was soft and racing away from the heft of the boat. I tried to stand and saw the shoreline slowly slipping away. The boat was taking on water and was slipping back into the ocean, soon to sink to the bottom offshore.

I let myself drop from the stairway to the door, then opened it and slid all the way down through the hold. When I reached the door and opened it, I heard helicopters in the distance and the sound of boats approaching fast. The Coast Guard was on their way, and I needed to escape in a hurry. I clasped the railing and crab-walked my way to an area of the ship away from the oncoming Coast Guard, and away from where I thought I would get dragged into the water.

"Sorry, buddy, this is going to suck," I apologized to Splinter as I patted his spot in my jacket and took off for the edge of the boat. As I leapt through the air and dove for the water, a voice filled my ear.

"What did she say?" I heard Archie ask right before I hit the surface.

CHAPTER FIVE

My body bobbed around in the water for what seemed like forever. My legs burned, and my shoulders felt like they might as well fall off, but I had to keep going. If nothing else, Splinter was on top of my back, I'm sure looking like a furry George Washington crossing the Delaware as I gasped and lurched my way through the water toward the far end of the beach. Glancing behind me gave me a little confidence none of the Coast Guard was after me, but it wasn't like I had a good reason for being out in the water fully clothed like I was. If they saw me, I would be toast.

The tip of my foot scraped sand, and I pushed a little harder until I could dig my knees into it and stay above the water. It felt so good to stop churning my legs that I sat like that for a moment before crawling up the beach to the shoreline. I crawled to an area where I felt like I wouldn't end up with water rushing over my head if the tide started coming in, and let myself crumple into the sand, then rolled onto my back.

Cold, exhausted, and pissed off, I tried to keep my

eyes open and not succumb to a nap, considering the soon-to-be roving Coast Guard looking for anyone who jumped off the ship. Hell, the rescue helicopter might have seen me already. I could only afford a few minutes before I had to get up and get moving. The water rushing up over my hips seemed to massage my legs, and although I detested water in my socks, for once I wasn't complaining. My eyes were drifting closer to closed, and I tried to rationalize it as I only needed to blink hard a couple of times.

"There she is," came a familiar voice from behind me, and the sound of feet thumping in the sand reached my ears. "Ugh, she smells like a sewer."

"That's the harbor, Archie," came a second voice.

That was Ally, and in my attempt to ignore reality, she was a piercing stab wound that popped the bubble and brought me back. I wanted to sleep, but Ally's voice was enough to bring me at least partway back.

"Let's get her out of the water," Archie directed, and I felt a pair of arms under my shoulders dragging me back, far up the beach and under the shade of an umbrella.

"Do you think she's okay?" Ally sounded worried.

"I'm fine," I croaked, convincing exactly no one, including myself.

"Yeah, you look it," Archie teased. "Smell it, too."

"Maybe I wouldn't smell like the harbor if my secret weapon didn't knock out all the electricity and make me need to jump off a damn boat, Archie," I shot back.

"Well, I mean, the name *is* Lights Out," he pointed out.

This was worthy of me opening my eyes, if only to scowl at him. He suddenly wanted to look anywhere at all other than at me. His attention was rapt on the bark on a nearby tree.

"Sorry," Archie mumbled under his breath.

"Help me up," I insisted, and Ally held out a hand for me to grab. I sat up, but when I tried to put pressure on my legs, they went to jelly again, and I fell hard on my ass. "Gonna need a minute for all that."

That was when I realized I was missing my tiny furry Washington. I searched around frantically, and Ally crouched down beside me to look around the sand.

"What? What is it?"

"Splinter. I can't find him. He was with me when I was crossing the water, but he's not here now," I told her.

"There he is," Archie announced and pointed.

I scrambled across the sand to where Splinter floated at the edge of the water. Face-down, arms and legs splayed out, he swirled around as the water flowed in and out. I forced myself to crawl over to him as worry tightened my throat and tears stung my eyes. The tide was taking him farther out, so I reached out to grab him by his fur and yank him to me.

As soon as his face came up out of the water, he screamed. I shoved him against my chest to quiet him, but when I pulled him away again, the sound came right back. I looked him in his little screaming face, gave him a fairly disgusting kiss, and shoved him into my pocket to freak out in privacy.

"He's fine," I reassured them.

"Hey, Slick, for reference, there's an outdoor shower right over there. In case you want to, you know," Ally suggested gently.

"Not stink?" I offered.

"Yeah," she agreed.

"Let me feel like my legs aren't made of water balloons and I'll get right on that. You don't happen to have any extra dry clothes, do you?"

"Be right back." She took off for the road.

After a few minutes, she returned with a plastic bag, and I groaned as I got to my feet. I shuffled to the outdoor shower, then hung the bag on the back of the door and turned on the water. Peeling off the wet clothes was refreshing all on its own, and some of the fog went away. The water was lukewarm, but it didn't matter.

"There's soap in the bag, Slick," Ally told me.

I opened it as I let the water cascade off my back. There was soap, all right. Along with a pair of black yoga pants a size too small and a t-shirt with a weird yellow creature in overalls and the saying 'I'd Rather Be Eating.' I had no clue what that was supposed to be, but the sentiment wasn't off. I shoved them back into the bag until I finished my shower.

When I finally finished and changed, then wrapped my still damp jacket around my weird shirt, we headed toward the boardwalk where the shops were now working over-time with the number of people who came to gawk at the overturned boat. I felt like food was in order, and Splinter agreed, having returned to my jacket pocket empty-handed.

We made our way to a small walk-up burger shack, and I stared at the menu in disappointment. I knew it was a burger shack, but part of me still hoped for a taco. Hell, I would've taken a snack-sized bag of Doritos. But, alas. I sat on a stool on the side of the long bar while Archie and Ally flanked me.

A TV droned on in the background with two talking heads blabbering about some peace summit between two major world leaders. I zoned it out, opting to focus more on the glass of water the cashier put in front of me, but some details filtered through. Something about Cabot in London, and how it was an extraordinary day for worldwide cooperation and a future of peace. *Yeah, right.* I had no idea how thirsty I was until right that moment. After downing the water in one gulp, I waved to get the waiter's attention and pointed at the glass.

"Bit thirsty, Miss?" He had a deeper southern drawl than one would expect in Jersey. It was disarming, and his mild, affable smile said more than his words could.

He was instantly the kind of guy I trusted to make me a sandwich because somehow, he would know how I'd like it. People like him littered diners and small restaurants the world over, and it was always a joy to find them. I nodded vigorously, and he smiled even wider as he took the glass and walked to the bar in the back where a large pitcher with ice sat.

"So, what's next?" Archie half-whispered. He clearly enjoyed the idea we might talk in code, but considering the afternoon I had, I didn't feel like concealing much of anything.

"The lizard-people trafficking was the only lead we had. Other than that, we need to keep a step ahead of the Guild Agents and keep our eyes peeled for anything that could relate to Hobbes," I told him.

"I haven't seen anything about him in a while. I hate to say it, but we might be stuck for a little," Ally added.

"Does it have to be in Jersey, though?" I asked.

Not that New Jersey was worse than any other place. It simply wasn't home. Or, what counted for home in my weird abandoned hotel with a Dog Man who kept an eye on the place and all of my stuff, which could fit into a small briefcase.

"We're only here because of the lizard people. You were the one who suggested you go save them from a life of slavery and whatever else they would use them for," Ally pointed out.

"Target practice?" Archie offered. I couldn't immediately tell if that was a terrible idea he thought someone would do or an idea he half-wanted to do himself.

"Who knows? At least I could help them," I said as the waiter came back to the table.

I made my order, and Archie and Ally made their much smaller orders. I watched with delight as the cook immediately fried our burgers and piled mine high with toppings of various types, including an onion ring right below the top bun.

"I think we ought to head out," Archie suggested between mouthfuls of fries. They were salty and delicious, and I likely could have eaten a meal of only them. "Especially after all the boat drama. I got a feeling the Philosophers Guild will put two and two together quickly enough to spell trouble for us."

"Probably. Last thing I want is to run into those guys again. Maybe we should head north? Go for the Canadian border? Or maybe south again, like Mexico," I offered.

"Or, we could stay one more day," Ally countered.

"Why in the hell would we do that?" Archie snapped.

"Well, there's a music festival tomorrow. And we need to have fun. Do you remember fun, Slick? We used to have it all the time," Ally teased.

"Oh, I remember fun. I also remember a night you tried to get me to have fun with you and I ended up with a station wagon in my front yard," I reminded her.

"If you had come, I wouldn't have had to come visit you, and the curb wouldn't have gotten in the way of my car," she argued.

"That curb had the right of way," I insisted.

"There would be none of that, Slick," she sang in a whimsical voice. "Only us, listening to music, having a few drinks and letting our hair down. Oh, and taco trucks. Taco trucks as far as the eye can see."

"Taco trucks!" I exclaimed, my attention officially caught.

"Sweet mother of mercy," Archie groaned.

"I'm in," I committed. "Who's headlining?"

CHAPTER SIX

As we walked through the gates of the festival, our freshly bought tickets in hand, a familiar thrill ran down my spine. Ally was right, I hadn't truly let loose and had fun in a long time, and now I had a chance to. I even changed out of my 'work' clothes after grabbing a few items Ally had bought for me that I kept in a plastic bag wherever I laid my head rather than ever wore.

Having clean new clothes was such a foreign concept after so long in The Deep that I wanted to hoard them. Today, I finally convinced myself this was a special occasion and donned the ripped jeans, tight tank top, and jersey combo of my youth. It was cute but still a little tomboyish, which fit the general motif I was discovering was my "look" now.

Archie chose to stay back at the mobile base, and as much as I enjoyed his cranky company, it was nice to be with Ally. It had taken a long talk with Ally to convince me to go, and she had argued vociferously that if I didn't occasionally do something fun, then what was the point of being alive? I was sure it was a teen movie monologue with a giant symphonic crescendo in her head, but for as silly and somewhat childish as she seemed while red-faced and hellbent on getting into cutoff shorts and primping her hair, she had a point.

There was nothing else for us to do at the moment, and Archie said he needed to get some supplies before we moved on anyway, which would take until tomorrow. We might as well go out and enjoy ourselves today and decompress a little before things got serious again. If nothing else, it kept Ally from exploding in cabin fever insanity.

Ever since I came back, it seemed like every moment together turned into either a prelude to or an actual life-or-death situation. There were very few times when it was the two of us not worrying about Fae creatures or Philosophers or some other thing bent on murdering one or both of us. At the music festival, it was only her and me picking up where we left off as kids.

We were a few feet inside the gates before I noticed the first of the Holy Grail monuments I came looking for—a taco truck named 'Avocado or Death.' I grabbed Ally by the elbow and pointed, and she sighed as she shook her head and smiled. I must have looked like a moron because Ally broke into a laugh and nodded.

"All right, we'll grab a taco first," she relented.

After satisfying my craving for the literal greatest food on earth, we made our way closer to the main stage area. The festival was huge, and people milled around all over the place. There were a few different stages set up around the park, and each one had its own lineup. I knew my tastes were so woefully out of the loop on popular music only a few of them seemed familiar, but then, I had never been the type to go crazy over a band anyway.

Ally, on the other hand, was beside herself. Apparently, a band she watched grow from small venues to now playing on the main stage would be here, and her entire ensemble was a collection of love letters to them. The entire way over, she explained how the denim shorts were a reference to the band's hit single about denim shorts before I zoned out a little. As we reached the main staging area, a beer vendor wandered by, and Ally stopped me.

"I don't know about you, but I could go for a drink."

"Sounds good," I responded and turned with her. Someone bumped into my arm from the side and muttered an apology, and the voice made my blood run cold. I looked up into the eyes of none other than Bentham.

She looked as shocked as I did. And different. Her hair teased out instead of in a tight ponytail like I saw every time I came across her. Also, makeup. A lot of makeup. A tight blouse and long capris completed a look I never thought I would see. Either this was the most elaborate and poorly thought out trap, or... No. It couldn't be Bentham on vacation. She looked ridiculous. Her eyes were round and her hand reached behind her as if to go for a gun.

She realized she wasn't in her usual uniform and I reached back for the switchblade but stopped before pulling it out. As much as I didn't trust anything about the situation, and would happily get rid of Bentham once and for all, gutting her in front of a few hundred concert-goers would likely cause a scene I wouldn't be able to escape from easily. We both stood there a moment, unsure of what to do next. Then Ally turned around with drinks in hand.

"I got two for each of us because I didn't want us to get thirsty later— Holy shit, what is she doing here?" she gasped.

"I'd like to know the same thing," I agreed, my voice low. Attracting the attention of the people in the area didn't rank high on my to-do list. Especially the police.

"Sara Slick, you need to come with me," Bentham instructed, her usual confident voice cracking a bit. She didn't have backup or a weapon and me coming with her either meant I went willingly, or she beat me hand-to-hand. For some reason, I didn't think she was terribly confident in either scenario. That gave me an edge.

"I'm not going anywhere. I'm innocent, and I have no reason to go anywhere with you," I told her.

Ally stood behind me and handed a beer over my shoulder into my hand. Then she leaned forward and offered one to Bentham, too.

"Maybe we could not make a scene in the middle of a very large music festival I've wanted to go to for years, all right?" Ally pleaded.

"It is my duty to—" Bentham began.

"You're at a concert. With two other people who also happen to be going to a concert. And one of them is offering you a nice, ice-cold beer. Perhaps you should take it and move on, and we will move on, and no one has to know about this exchange but the three of us."

"You know I can't do that, Slick," Bentham shot back. "I can't shut off being a Guild Agent any more than you can shake off being the Heinous Sara Slick. Who, by the way, made a hell of a splash in West Virginia."

"I helped those people." My voice dropped an octave. If she planned on making what happened there an example of my guilt, I wouldn't worry about the people around us anymore. I would beat her senseless right here.

"That's what was so strange," she replied, a hint of accusation in her voice. "By the time we got there, everything was settled. Burned all to hell, but settled. And anyone we talked to about the girl named Slick had nothing but good words. Glowing words. Really, unbelievably fantastic words. You did something good there, and I can acknowledge that. Why?"

An Agent of the Guild admitting someone like me could be anything less than the worst thing to ever happen to existence as a whole was pretty impressive. Maybe it was the capris. They were so tight they cut off the blood flow to her brain. Still, I didn't appreciate the tone or her questioning my motives.

"I helped people who needed help, and the people there painted a different picture of me than you expected. Maybe that should tell you something." It was more of a statement than a question. Bentham looked down at the beer bottle Ally held out to her. She reached up and snatched it from her, brought it to her lips, and downed a few big gulps without ever breaking eye contact.

"It doesn't change my job, Slick," she told me. "I have to bring you in. I don't get the whole Good Samaritan routine you have going, but it doesn't absolve what you and I both know you did."

"What you *think* I did. I'm innocent. But I don't think

you can take me in without me volunteering, and that isn't happening. And you can't brain-wipe ten thousand people, so..." I edged a little away from her. "I think Ally and I will enjoy the show. You should, too. Way the hell over there."

A loud, blaring guitar, followed by feedback that made everyone clench their jaws and cover their ears, reverberated in the air. Bentham instinctively turned toward the stage where the sound came from, and I grabbed Ally's hand and we took off into the crowd. Bentham stood there a moment, then seemed to clear her head by shaking it and came after us. If she wanted to get me, she would have to do it the hard way. A really hard way.

I aimed for the front of the crowd and pushed my way past fans of every type until I got where I wanted. The band on stage was thankfully one I knew of, and if I timed this right, I could get us out of here. A few bars into their next song, a circle opened wide around us. The mosh pit began.

Soon, people of all sizes were running, jumping, and shoving their way around the pit while the music blared around us. I kept my eyes on the crowd, spinning around like my head was on a swivel, looking for anything that might indicate we were trapped. I scanned the crowd but saw nothing but the usual concert-goers, mostly drunk and entirely unconcerned about two girls ducking through the pit. Off to the side, a security guard was backing almost into the pit himself while yelling at a group of kids who were climbing on top of a temporary art installation that for all the world looked like a man peeing on a fish.

Bentham tried to get in the pit by elbowing her way past a few larger boys, but was totally out of her element and watched helplessly as Ally and I shoved our way to the other side. The security guard, now in the middle of what he must have assumed was a fistfight, started yelling over the music at the shoving, dancing kids.

I watched over my shoulder as a wall of boys banging their heads, swallowed Bentham, then I ducked, and we disappeared into the crowd while snaking back to one of the exits and out of the park.

"Sorry I couldn't stick around, Ally," I apologized as we took off on foot out of the area.

"It's cool. I'm used to hanging out with you ending in life-or-death situations," she forgave.

I knew she meant it as a joke, but it stung me. She was right. I was dragging my friend through every kind of danger imaginable, and she was trying to live a normal life. If we got out of this alive, I owed her a hundred years of tacos, concerts, and karaoke.

CHAPTER SEVEN

"I'm telling you, this thing needs a name," I commented.

Ally looked at the beaten-up RV after taking a few steps back to take in all its glory. All its forty-year-old fucked-up-tuna-can Transformer glory.

"Well," she said, "the Batmobile is taken. Ditto on the Mystery Machine. Same with Kitty."

"Kit," Archie corrected as he opened the door and climbed into the RV.

"What?" Ally asked.

"KITT. The car's name is KITT. Not Kitty. From the show *Knight Rider*. It stood for Knight Industries Two Thousand. Then later, Knight Industries Three Thousand, but that was during the new series," Archie clarified.

"Why do you know that?" I asked.

Archie shrugged. "Sometimes I get wrapped up in making runes late into the night and end up watching reruns. Humans fascinate me."

"So you watch science fiction?" Ally asked.

"I mean, technically it's not science fiction," Archie pointed out.

"All right, we can continue this riveting conversation inside the mobile task force base," I told them.

"Oooh, that should be its name," Ally suggested when we got the rest of the way into the RV and Archie closed the door behind us.

"That's not its name, that's its title. It's what it is," I pointed out.

"Isn't that what a name is?" Ally asked.

Archie latched the door and triggered the switch he'd installed on the wall to open a panel toward the back of the vehicle. What used to unfold into a Murphy bed became his tiny lab space, complete with jars and bottles of various materials attached to the walls with Velcro straps.

"No," I argued. "It's like me. My *name* is Sara Slick. I *am* an epic, legendary Near-born, Far-trained badass."

"See? Humans are fascinating," Archie repeated.

Ally laughed and climbed into the front seat. She hit a few buttons to activate the customizations Archie had put in place for her. The seat adjusted to her body, forming to her and supporting her legs so she was essentially sitting in a recliner with the pedals raised to meet her feet.

Archie said it was the cutting edge of comfort and ergonomic support during long stretches of driving. I thought it was the ideal way to put Ally to sleep while she should be driving us, and the cutting edge would most likely be the windshield shards flying at me during the impact.

But what did I know? Ally had been driving for more than ten years, and the closest thing I had to my license was memories of a pissed off behind-the-wheel instructor for my two hours of instruction before I stopped, and a souvenir ID from my sister's birthday party at Chuck E. Cheese a few months before the Philosophers snatched me.

Archie walked over to his lab and stood in the middle of the circular panel inset into the floor. He reached down and latched his feet into place, then released the lock that kept the circle from moving. Now he could spin around freely and access all points of his lab while staying securely in place as the RV moved. Him twisting back and forth and spinning around looked like something out of an '80s music video created by someone with a geek edge and far too much pep in their step. But so far, he hadn't toppled over while in mid-run creation, so I took that as a good thing.

"You all locked and loaded back there?" Ally called while peering at Archie in the rearview mirror.

He waved at her. "Light her up."

"Not the words I want used in reference to the vehicle I'm in," I muttered.

"Turn her ignition gently, then responsibly and in full compliance with all local laws and regulations, proceed on the intended path of travel," he amended.

"Are you good, Slick?" Ally asked.

I dropped to the floor and pulled my knees up, then crossed my arms over my chest. "Yep. Going to do some sit-ups on the road."

"Nothing says leisurely road travel like lying on the floor doing a bunch of sit-ups," she replied.

"Gotta stay strong. You never know when the next time

will come that we have to beat the snot out of a Fae or save people from burning buildings." I did several sit-ups, then added in a few twists for good measure.

If only those were euphemisms and not direct references to things we had actually had to do in the not too distant past.

"So, we're going to pretend you didn't almost get your ass captured by that Guild Agent with the apparent identity confusion?" Ally asked.

"Yeah, where was her buddy? The mean one with the big fists." Archie punched the air.

"That would be Thrash and, no, we are definitely not pretending that. That was not my favorite way ever to end a day at a festival. I didn't even get to don socially irresponsible clothing and dance like I popped my brain in an Easy-Bake Oven." Silver lining.

"So, are we going to talk about it?" Ally asked.

"Just because I'm not ignoring it doesn't mean I want to talk about it. That was shaving things a little too close. Splinter hasn't even come out of my pocket. I think he's still playing dead," I guessed.

Right on cue, Splinter squeezed himself out of my pocket and ran across the RV to the kitchenette. This was another part of the vehicle given a boost by Archie. My little rodent toilet brush had his favorite part. He used it now as he scrambled up a ramp built into the side of the counter and cabinet and through a flap that led to his favorite foods. He could have stayed in there and coated himself in cheese doodle dust to his heart's content, but that wasn't his style. He knew a person in distress when he saw one.

His butt emerged first, and he barely made the tight turn to change direction and make his way back down to me while dragging a bag of sweet potato chips. He climbed up on my chest, pulled a chip out with his mouth, and offered it to me.

"Is your weird rat thing feeding you because you're exercising?" Ally asked.

"He chose sweet potato chips. At least he's trying to be healthy," I defended my sweet Splinter.

I was sure there was another snide remark and a potential Bubonic plague reference coming, but we didn't get to hear it. A sound from somewhere in the back of the RV made everyone fall silent. We listened and heard the sound again, something between a scrape and a knock.

"What's that?" Archie whispered while turning his head to keep his eyes locked on me as his circle responded to a wide turn and sent him around in the other direction.

I shook my head as I carefully set Splinter aside and stood. "It's Bentham. I'd put money on it. I'm going to find her."

My hand wrapped around a bat sitting on the couch. It wasn't as elegant or impressive as some of the runes Archie created for me, or the perfect switchblade Solon had crafted, but it would do its job if the need arose. I made my way to one of the two bedrooms in the back of the RV, where I was pretty sure the sound originated. It came again, and I turned to the narrow closet. The door shook, and I tightened my grip on the bat. I reached for the handle, flung open the door, and swung the bat at the same time.

The bat sliced right through the air and smashed

through the closet door. The form that had been inside the closet ducked out of the way and ran across the room. I screamed and ran after it. As we burst into the front of the RV, Archie shouted and tried to lunge for the hooded creature. Unfortunately for him, he forgot his feet were attached to his anchor mechanism and ended up in a heap on the floor. The RV swayed back and forth as Ally tried to keep it together while still driving.

I lifted the bat again and stepped forward to bring it down on the intruder's head when it whipped around. The hood fell back in time for me to divert the bat and smash the hell out of the corner of the table rather than the scaly green skull in front of me. I'd seen that face before. It stared back at me with wide, frantic eyes.

"You're one of the Lizard People I rescued." She looked so young, far too young to stow away in strange RVs, although I didn't know if there was actually an appropriate age for that to happen. "What are you doing here?"

She rushed forward the few steps to close the space between us so we were only a few inches apart.

"I came to warn you. The world is ending!"

CHAPTER EIGHT

I blinked at the small green girl a few times. Her wide-eyed expression didn't change. I closed my eyes and leaned my ear toward her to improve my concentration.

"I'm sorry. What now?" I asked.

"The world. It's ending. I had to come warn you," she announced as earnestly as before.

I nodded. "Yep. That's what I thought you said." I let out a sigh and opened my eyes to look at her. "I'm sorry if we don't immediately have a huge reaction to your announcement. We've kind of been through that for real, so we take it pretty seriously."

"This is for real," she insisted. "I heard the bad guys who kidnapped us talking about it."

A feeling like cold water rushed down my back, and after the round of work Archie put into the big tuna can a couple of weeks back, I knew it wasn't the air conditioner leaking. She really was worried about something. I nodded toward the couch behind her.

"Why don't we sit down and backtrack a little. Start

with the basics and we'll see where we end up," I suggested. She nodded, and we sat on the couch. "I'm Sara Slick."

"I know."

I cringed. "Oh. Yeah." I put my hands up in the air beside my head and made a mock screaming sound. "Smooth first impression."

"I'm sorry about that," she offered.

"Nope. Not at all. It's fine. I have to remember you don't think the same things I do when I hear my name. I think about my father and my grandmother and Ally giving me my nickname. You think of mass murder and mayhem." I move my hands up and down at my sides like a scale. "You have to weigh all the perspectives."

"Right." She extended one clawed hand toward me. "I'm Pip."

My eyes widened, and I grinned as I shook it. "Pip? Like the character in that book they made me read in middle school?"

Pip extended her arms in front of her and examined them. "I really don't know. I didn't go to middle school."

"Don't," I recommended. "That's a few years out of my life I definitely wouldn't ever want to relive. Those people can be mean."

I shuddered, but Pip didn't smile.

"You're doing it, too." Her voice sounded disappointed and faintly sad.

I glanced around, not realizing I had done anything. "What? What did I do?"

Pip let out a sigh. "People always think I'm younger or talk to me like I'm stupid or couldn't possibly understand anybody—even my family. I mean, they know how old I am, but they don't put a lot of value in me. Because I'm tiny even for a Lizard Person, they think I'm not good enough. They wouldn't listen to me when I told them what I heard. That's why I had to find you. I knew you would listen to me and know what to do."

"Okay, first, did you call yourself a Lizard Person?" She quietly nodded. I continued, "That can't be what your kind is called."

The edges of Pip's mouth turned up, almost in a smile. "Sure. We tried introducing ourselves by our proper names to what humans we had contact with for years. It's nearly unintelligible."

"Fair enough." I nodded. "And I'm sorry. I don't think you have no value. I mean, I just met you, but I see good potential."

She smiled fully. "Thanks."

"Speaking of which. Why were you in the closet?"

"It was somewhere to hang out. I got stuck, though. Anyway. I don't know everything. They didn't lay it all out and hand out blueprints or anything, but I caught some of it, and what I caught definitely doesn't sound good."

"What did you hear?"

Splinter came and sat beside me, shoving sweet potato chips in his mouth as he readied himself for the story ahead.

"Something is going down at the peace summit. Something involving Senator Cabot," Pip told me.

"Senator Cabot?" I asked. "That name sounds familiar. I don't know why, since I'm a little behind on world affairs, heh," I joked. No one laughed. I sighed.

"She's a senator, and she's been spearheading this peace

accord for months," Ally informed me. "It's a big deal, and there will be representatives from all the major U.N. nations there. She's on the fast track to a run at being President if this thing goes well."

"Do you think she could be in danger?" I asked. "Why would Farsiders have anything to do with a Senator?"

"I don't know," Pip admitted. "But it's something. Something big. The people who kidnapped us weren't involved in the plan, but they knew about it. That's why they started kidnapping so many of us. They were preparing for war—and they think it's imminent."

Well, shit.

"I think it's about time for a brief pit stop," Ally announced an hour later.

We'd all stayed quiet, pulling inside ourselves as we tried to process what Pip told us. It was a lot to process. If Pip was right, the Farsiders capturing the Lizard folk were banking on a lot of chaos and war if their plan worked out, and the snickering schemers had mentioned Cabot by name. They were downright giddy about it and about all the things they would get away with in broad daylight after their plan worked and the summit went south.

Ally and I stayed quiet. The young lizard girl, not so much. And by extension, not Archie. She spent up until about twenty minutes ago playing with Splinter as he ran around, bounced off cushions, and skittered across the counter. Finally, he tumbled from the back of the couch and landed on the gray cushions already deep in sleep.

That was when she wandered over to Archie and started trying to figure out what he was up to.

"What's this?"

"Hairs."

"And this?"

Archie set his jaw. "Scales from a Far sea monster."

"What are these?" Pip pointed.

"River rocks." He was trying to keep the aggravation out of his voice and not doing well.

And so it continued, a cascade of questions and nosiness, answered by an increasingly grumpy Archie. I felt like Ally and I managed to de-grump him so much, but a few minutes strapped to the floor of an RV with a tiny lizard girl rattling off every thought that came to her mind in her existence stuffed it right back in. He seemed the most relieved when Ally suggested the pit stop and immediately crouched to release his feet from the spinning circle and secure the panel in place.

The RV pulled into a rest stop along the turnpike. When I stepped out into the fresh air, I noticed an over-look. We'd hit one of those rare and illustrious times when a clean, well-equipped rest stop with a fabulous view wasn't swarming with tourists and road trippers. Archie headed to the bathroom, and Ally and Pip made their way to the vending machines.

If there was one thing Ally couldn't resist during a road trip, it was a vending machine. When we were younger, she used to keep a zippered bag full of quarters in the glove compartment in case she pulled off at a rest stop. No other vending machine would do. It had to be a rest stop during a road trip, possibly one in a hotel in certain circumstances.

I left Splinter sleeping in a little ball and headed to the overlook by myself. I wanted a few moments to breathe and let everything sink into my mind. The sheer enormity of the world took my breath away as I looked out at the view. I wondered how many times I'd seen this exact scene or one like it and didn't bother to notice it. After escaping The Deep, I never wanted that to happen again. I couldn't take anything for granted anymore, and the ten years in the filthy, cramped, subterranean prison made everything look so big.

The view stretched out in front of me like it went on forever. It was beautiful with the sun streaming through it that I wanted to reach out and touch it. My mind wandered to Solon. I was trying to imagine what he would think of this scenery and me standing in it when Ally walked up.

"What are you thinking about over here all by yourself, Slick? If there's a way to consider Pip a travel accessory and keep her in the glove compartment?"

"I hadn't quite gotten there yet, but I'll stand behind that choice. I'm thinking about Solon."

"You haven't told me much about him," Ally led.

"There wasn't a ton to tell." I sighed. "I don't think I knew a lot about him. Some, obviously. We spent a lot of time together, but he was always very…well, guarded about himself."

"Then why did he help you? You didn't tell me why he saved you or why he put so much sacrifice into training you." She turned and leaned against the railing.

I shook my head slightly. "I never found out. He never explained why he saved me or why he spent so much time with me, training me. I was a loyal student, and he was a great teacher, but talking about his thoughts and feelings wasn't exactly his strong point. He was so mysterious. But I'd like to think he would be proud of me for what I've done."

She turned back to sling her arm around my shoulders and squeeze me close.

"Of course, he is. You've taken all his training and brought it to a new level. He would think you're incredible, Slick. Something all of us already know," she teased.

I sighed and let my head rest on her shoulder as we continued to stare out over the view.

"What are we going to do?" I eventually asked.

"What do you mean?" she asked.

"About the end of the world. We can't go to the cops. We'd end up with our recorded phone conversation with the dispatcher splashed all over every news channel. And if they did believe us, they wouldn't have any way to help us. I can't go to the Philosophers. Their field agents are after me, and Bentham made it clear they're still very much coming for me."

"What are you saying?" She rested her head against mine briefly.

I lifted my head off her shoulder. "There's no one who can stop this but us."

"Can we do it? Can we stay strong enough?" Ally asked.

I rested my head against hers. "I don't know. But we have to try."

CHAPTER NINE

Archie blinked at me a few times. I could tell he wasn't quite on the train with me, yet. I did my best to explain the plan formulating in my head, but it seemed the formulation wasn't quite finished and he didn't pick up on the fine nuances of what I had in mind. Either that, or there weren't any fine nuances and I had no idea what I was talking about. I went with the first option to keep myself trucking along.

"Explain that to me one more time," he said.

"She thinks we should go to the peace summit," Pip told him.

He nodded. "No, I got that. I'm not sure I got the rest of it."

There wasn't really a rest of it. But if there was one thing I was good at, it was faking it 'til I made it.

"We'll fly to the summit, try to contact Senator Cabot, then hopefully explain the situation. From there, we rescue her and save the world," I concluded.

"Just like that, huh?"

"Essentially." I gave a matter-of-fact nod.

So, it wasn't the most thought-out and detailed of plans ever created. I didn't have a lot of time to work on it. And for short notice, I thought it was brilliant.

"What I don't understand is what Senator Cabot has to do with any of this," Ally pointed out. "Why would Hobbes and any of his creepy little minions want her? Don't they usually go for a more blunt approach to utter chaos and destruction? Political espionage is outright weird for them."

"Yes, but that hasn't really worked out for them so far. Not against us." I let out a sigh and the shoulders I had pulled back proudly sagged a little. "I wanted that to sound a lot more compelling than it did."

"I thought it was compelling," Pip offered. "You're like your very own group of superheroes!"

"Not the first time we've heard that," I commented. "I appreciate the fangirl support, but it looks more and more like us being able to ward off the Farsiders Hobbes has in his pocket has only resulted in him latching onto humans. I didn't escape from the Deep and go after the Guild and Hobbes to serve up humans on a silver platter, and this will move so many more people into his camp."

Archie cringed. "I know that's a metaphor for you, but I know some people who would be very interested in that proposition. Maybe we should use a different analogy."

I looked at him for a long second. "Gross. But, fine. I didn't go through all that to make it here so they could destroy the human world like this."

"I thought your whole reason for escaping from prison was to clear your name," Ally said.

"Hurtful, Ally." She tilted her head at me, unconvinced by my wide, innocent eyes. "I army-crawled and Philosopher-bashed my way out of Hell's timeout closet to figure out why they framed my father for heinous crimes, but it's not only about that. Now that I know how big this thing really is, I can't let it keep going. Hobbes is ready to take out the world. I can't let that happen. There is too much good left in this world. Too much happiness and beauty and love and amazement."

"And tacos," Archie added.

"Yes, Archie, thank you," I acknowledged. "And tacos. There might be a lot of nasty grimy bad shit that happens every day, but it's not enough to make the world not worth existing. I don't know who the fuck Hobbes thinks he is, but he won't blot out all of existence on my watch."

"Yaaaaaaaay!" Pip cheered.

"Okay, Norma Ray. That was inspiring, but it didn't really answer my question. Why would Hobbes want to attack Cabot? This peace summit has nothing to do with Farsiders. If anything, it could alert the world's leaders to them if they attacked. Why would Hobbes want to bring the heat of the entire planet down on himself?" Ally asked.

"Maybe that's the point. Senator Cabot is a respected leader. People will look at her for insight and motivation. Maybe everyone's waiting for something amazing to happen. That's how politicians roll. They'll hang out in the background all quiet and unassuming, shaking hands, signing papers, kissing babies and then BAM," I threw my hands out in a sharp gesture, "they're playing Flight of the Valkyries while moseying down the street in a tank. It's all about the anticipation."

"It's a peace summit, Slick. I don't think it will involve any tanks," Ally pointed out.

"Even so. This is the perfect time for her to emerge triumphant and make a big impact. Maybe that's what everyone is expecting. All the attention will be on her, so when Hobbes attacks, it will be public and dramatic, and it would be so demoralizing for Hobbes to destroy a peace summit that a war between The Far and The Near would start out with The Far having the psychological advantage. Pip already said the baddies are preparing for war. It's coming soon, and they'll want to make a big deal out of it. This is their opening salvo, and we need to be there to stop it. Otherwise, not only will Cabot get hurt, but the war between The Far and The Near will start with them drawing first blood."

"All right," Archie said with a bit of an edge to his voice. "I guess it's settled. Let's get ready. What kind of gear will we need for this plan?"

"Isn't that kind of your jam? You're our gear dude." I waved my hand at him like I was anointing him.

His eyes slid over to me and I quickly realized he didn't appreciate his new unofficial title. I would have to keep working on it.

"I can't spontaneously come up with a list of things we need for something when I don't know exactly what we'll have to do." Grumpy Archie wasn't letting up.

"I haven't exactly made it a habit to attend peace summits, Archie, so I don't really know what to expect," I told him.

"Great. Well, I can come up with a list of basic materials that would help us in a wide range of situations. I can't guarantee it will contain everything we might need, but it will give us a good chance. Of course, sourcing those things is a different story," he warned.

"What do you mean?" I asked.

"It won't be easy. The number of quality people who are willing to sell to us is dwindling. It probably doesn't come as much of a surprise to you that we're developing a bit of a reputation. There aren't a lot of dealers around who want their names tied up with Sara Slick," he pointed out.

"Okay. Well, that's too bad for them." I wanted to hit an emphatic pose but couldn't think of one that wouldn't make me feel like Peter Pan.

"It's too bad for us, too. We can't simply stroll into the grocery store and ask them where their Farstuff department is," Archie snipped.

"But we *can* rely on them to have a good supply of Nearstuff." I grinned at him.

His grumpy face didn't change. "Silver lining."

I sagged a little. "We need this, Archie. We've been flailing around for how long now? We're trying to bring Hobbes down before he can wipe out life as we know it, and right now, the best we have to go on is what Pip heard. It might not make sense to us, but we don't really have the luxury of choosing what we follow-up on. If we don't do this, it could be disastrous."

"All right," he gave in. "I can give you a list of the supplies we need before we travel. It'll take at least a few days to get everything, then probably another couple of days to get there if we want to stay under the radar."

He walked back to his lab and pulled a pad of paper and pen from a drawer. While hunched over the counter, he started scribbling, tore off the page, and scribbled on another. This didn't seem like it would be a super-fast process, so I turned to Pip. The young Lizard Person sat at the edge of the cushion on the couch, primed and ready for whatever would happen. She didn't seem anxious or worried, but more excited about what was coming.

Her little green head turned and glanced around as she took in all the details of our customized RV.

"Pip?" I leaned slightly toward her.

"Hmm?" Her eyes snapped to me like she almost forgot I was there beside her.

"You doing okay? With all this?" I gestured around to encompass Archie, Ally, and me.

She smiled. "Absolutely. This place is great. I've never seen anything like it."

"No one has ever seen anything like it," Ally commented.

"I meant the whole your species getting kidnapped and facing down an impending war thing," I clarified.

"Oh." Her smile faltered a little, and her eyes moved to stare directly in front of her. She thought for a few seconds, and there was no sound in the RV except Archie scratching away at the paper. "Um. Yeah. I'm okay. I'm glad I was able to find you. Now that I have, I know everything will be all right."

"So," I began, trying to figure out how to delicately broach the subject, "is there anywhere you would want us to drop you off?"

"Drop me off?" she asked.

"I mean, you obviously can't come with us—"

"Why not?" she interjected, her hands going to her hips

and an edge creeping into her voice before backing down a little. "You could use someone like me, you know? Besides, I hate my family, and humans are difficult to be around without wanting to gnaw their faces off. Present company excluded."

"Thanks?" Ally cocked her head to the side.

"I mean, most humans suck almost as much as my family. No one in The Far is friendly to people like me. Plus, I really like the idea of doing something good for once. And here you are, Sara Slick, saving the universe. I want to be part of that." She blinked.

No pressure.

"All right. I have the lists," Archie announced.

I was still locked in a staring contest with Pip, who stared imploringly back. Finally, I nodded once, and a smile stretched across her face. Despite myself, a small smile stretched across mine too. I turned to Archie.

"Lists? With an 's?'" I asked.

"Yeah. I told you, since I don't know exactly what's going on or what we should expect, I don't know everything we'll need. I came up with the best list of Nearsider stuff and Farsider stuff I could. It's a little random, but it will give me the flexibility I need. With these things, I can make a bunch of different stuff depending on what we end up encountering. But that means it's not a short list and if we want to head to the summit anytime soon, we need to divide and conquer."

"Go, team. So, who's doing what?" I asked.

"Ally, I have you doing the Nearsider stuff. Follow the list and bring back everything you can get your hands on," he instructed. "I really need the top ten things there, and we may as well not go if I can't get them. Everything else ranges from necessary, but maybe I can find there, to something to keep Pip quiet while I do something important."

He offered a page to Ally, who took it and scanned it.

She nodded. "Duct tape, kitchen shears, a pack of twelve-volt batteries… I get those. But the heels off a pair of stilettos? A blue-eyed teddy bear? Fourteen green M&Ms? A melon-baller?"

"I need it," Archie said weakly.

"Why?" I asked.

"I just do."

There was a moment of uncomfortable silence before Ally shook her head.

"Okay, fine, yeah. I can get this stuff," she said.

"Great. Slick, you're on *Farsider* stuff." He held a list out to me.

"Of course, I am." I snatched the paper from his hand and looked at it. "What else would you make me do?"

"You're more familiar with these things than Ally is. You're also more comfortable dealing with the type of people who sell them," he explained.

"And what are you going to get?" I looked around, trying to find his list.

"Passports."

"Passports," I repeated flatly.

"Do you have one?" He gave me a smug look.

I opened my mouth, then closed it. "No."

"Neither do I. Neither does Pip." He gestured at the lizard girl, who smiled.

"I do." Ally lifted one hand.

Archie pointed at her. "Still getting you a fake one. We don't want anyone able to track us. I know someone who makes passports for Farsiders all the time. It's a common need for us. We can't get real identification, so we always need fakes. He'll make us ones that we can use for the flight and access to the peace summit."

"I'll come with you!" Pip exclaimed. "I want to come up with my fake name."

"You don't have to have a fake name," he told her.

"But I want one." Her pout almost made her adorable.

"Okay. You can have a fake name," Archie relented, already exasperated by his biggest fan.

He looked over at me, his eyes pleading for me to pry her away from him and take her with me. I grinned.

"Have a great time! Meet back here soon." I hopped up and bounced out of the RV, only to return a second later. "I'll probably need a ride. And to know where I'm going."

CHAPTER TEN

Why is it always a creepy building? Why couldn't it be a beach-front hotel? Or a fun indie arcade? No, it's always a fucking creepy building where I can smell the mold from a block away, and even the birds avoid it.

I kicked an empty can of bottom-shelf beer out of my way as I continued toward the creep-tastic building in a slow, methodical stomp. Yet another out of the way, abandoned building where absolutely nothing good can happen, and surrounded by the depressing aftereffects of a local economy drying up.

Every single time.

I needed Archie to find some friends who worked in Hawaii or in the business section of a major metropolitan city. This was getting depressing. It didn't help that Archie framed this particular dealer as 'more or less reputable.' Which was code for, 'I have no idea if you're walking into Murdertown's Most Wanted or a place where you can buy what you need and maybe ice cream.'

As usual, this building looked abandoned. Short, squat,

and entirely industrial, it looked like a cover model for 'Depressing Buildings Monthly.' A small whiff of smoke rose from one of the exhaust pipes for what must be an ancient oil-burning system and poured out of the top of the building. Other than that, it looked empty, which in my experience usually meant hordes of Farsiders, or agents looking to arrest me.

I muttered a few more curses to myself as I walked the perimeter of the building to check for mysterious vehicles or giant gangs of Fae hanging around. When none of them appeared, I relaxed a little and made my way to the back door Archie suggested I use.

The door, like most doors in industrial buildings used as a front for dealers of all kinds, was propped open. Archie's instructions were to go in that open door, make my way right until I ran into the far wall and turn left, then right. At that point, I should arrive at a large open space where a desk would be standing in the middle and the guy I came to meet would be sitting. Archie described him as a 'bookworm' type, although one who was well-connected.

I followed the directions Archie gave me. When I made the last turn, I saw the table in the center of the room. It was a warehouse area, and surprisingly clean, and the table was neat and organized, but no one sat in the chair. I was about to step forward when the patter of canine feet surprised me and I turned to see Dog. Our eyes met, and he yanked his head back toward the door. He must have followed me in here. A thousand questions whirled through my mind all at once.

"What is it? And where the hell have you been? How did you find me?"

Dog barked, answering exactly none of my pressing questions. The sound reverberated off the walls, but he didn't step forward. He looked back toward the entrance again and looked back at me.

"I'm sorry, buddy, but I have a job to d—" I began. A loud yell like someone was being hurt cut me off. I turned to it, and Dog ran around me to block my path. He began barking loudly and growling.

"Shit, I've gotta go help." I ran, leaving Dog barking behind me. The sound came from deep in the warehouse where the lights were off. My thoughts immediately went to some nerdy guy, waiting around for me to show up, and breaking his leg stocking some shelf. That would be my luck, for someone to get hurt on the most mundane of missions.

As I got farther from the lit area, I slowed down. The yell had stopped and now there was only a soft whimpering, but it wasn't coming from somewhere I could identify. It was like it was all around me, somewhere the sound could push down. Like above. I looked up and stepped back in horror. There was someone tall and lanky and, from the looks of it, a fairy, hanging from one of the tall metal shelves. Around his neck was a crude noose made out of what looked like a spool of barbed wire. Blood dripped down his shirt, off his shoes and onto the floor.

"Oh, God, I'm coming!" I assured him and grabbed the shelving. I climbed up by stepping on boxes I hoped would support my weight and wished I'd done more rock-climbing in my time since imprisonment. Or before my imprisonment. Or at any point in my life.

I reached for his shoes and briefly tried to lift him, so it could create slack, but realized it was no use. He was passing out and not capable of the dexterity it would take to get out of the wire once he had it loose. Not to mention, his hands looked like they might be bound behind his back too. I climbed another shelf higher and saw his hands were, indeed, also bound at the wrist with barbed wire.

I shuddered at the thought of who would do that to someone, then realized this guy dealt in Farside weapons. Any number of the Farsiders who imprisoned me in The Deep would do something like this and consider it the day's entertainment.

Not today.

I got up onto the shelf by his waist and looked up. The noose was on the shelf right above and was tied tight to his neck, meaning he wasn't hanging by much of the wire. If I could sever the barbed restraint, it would be risky letting him fall, but it would relieve the pressure and the cutting of his neck and might save him. I knew my switchblade would slice through the noose, and as soon as I climbed on top of the top shelf, I pulled it out and wedged it under the wire between it and the shelf pole. It cut the restraints smoothly as I yanked up, and the man's body dropped legs-first to the floor.

He cried out when he landed, then began coughing hard. I whipped around to climb back down the shelves. When I reached him, he was in tremendous pain. Blood poured from his neck where the barbs ripped his skin as he fell, and from the puncture wounds where it dug into him while he hung. An entire piece of skin from his neck was missing and a glance upward saw it hanging from one of the prongs on the wire.

I reached over him and cut the wire binding his hands and tossed it away, then frantically looked around for something to stop the bleeding. It pooled around his head like a crimson halo, and I knew he didn't have long before blood loss would make him pass out again.

Finding a bag of surprisingly normal white t-shirts among the shelves was lucky and unexpected. I ripped open the packaging, pulled out one of the shirts and went to work cutting it into strips. When I got the first strip cut off, I wrapped it around the fairy's neck and grabbed the second.

I tried to hold the fabric to him to stop the bleeding, but I knew it wouldn't take long. He was bleeding quite badly and needed to get to a hospital soon. Since I didn't think he would want police here, that meant I needed to help him, and get him out of the building.

"Okay, dude, I'm going to help you up now so we can get you out of here."

He sputtered something I couldn't understand, and I cocked my head to one side.

"Sorry, I don't understand you, buddy. I don't think you should try to talk though, okay? So let's get you out of here." I tried to move faster.

"Trap," he forced out. "It's a trap."

A sound caused my spine to straighten and every hair on my neck to stand on end. It was a hiss. Not simply any hiss, but the hiss of a being who has two large fangs and likes to see people drained of their blood. I turned to face the sound but saw only shadows. The vampires I fought before were simple creatures, and it confused me why one would go through all the trouble of setting up a trap. They didn't seem that intelligent.

It all made sense when the being stepped tentatively into the light, long dark shadows casting down his face and body and obscuring much of him. A finely tailored shoe being joined by a second stepped into view. Pressed pants and a designer black shirt with a red tie appeared before what I could see of the face. When I could, it took me aback, and I tried to steel myself for whatever was next.

It looked like a man, with two long, impressive fangs, and dark black hair pulled back into a tight ponytail. It eyed me with satisfaction, then looked around again, as if searching for my friends. When it saw none, its expression turned to one of slight disappointment, and its arm came from behind it. In its hand, it carried a fencing sword, which it brought to its forehead, then down and away in a swooshing sound. Archie had told me about ones like this, but I didn't believe it. This was no mere vampire.

This was a Varkolak.

CHAPTER ELEVEN

"Sara Slick." The creature had a slight lisp when he said my name. It seemed like an accent hid deep in his voice as well, but I couldn't make it out.

"I don't know who you are, or what your game is, but I am getting this guy out of here right now, and if you so much as move..." I stepped toward him.

"You will what? Exactly?" Under his long, hooked nose, his mouth stretched impossibly wide, showing his wide array of gleaming white teeth. Especially the long ones. "You will attack me with that blade of yours? A toy." He waved his arm. When he did so, the blade yanked in that direction. I tried to hold it firm, but the pull was too great, and it flew out of my fingers and clattered on the floor.

"What the hell?" I demanded.

"You are but a child, Slick. A tiny gnat on the grandness of the world, and yet..." he stepped toward me, and although everything in my brain screamed to run, I felt locked into place. It was as if his eyes held some special power over me, and I couldn't look away. I was transfixed by how impossibly blue they were, and how they seemed to grow and recede, like they were reacting to the beating of a heart.

My heart.

I felt it in my chest, thrashing against my ribcage, pumping blood through my system, trying to give my body the fuel it needed to move, but instead it made me hot. I began to sweat, and still I couldn't move. His eyes, expanding and shrinking with the beat of my heart, seemed not to look directly into mine. They stared lower, off to the side. Near my neck. I tried to close my eyes and break the spell and found it almost impossible to do.

"Who are you?" I sputtered while forcing one eye closed and feeling the tiniest twinge of relief. If I could only get the other closed too.

"My name is too complicated for your human mouth."

"I've gotten that a lot lately," I shot.

"But I shall allow you to know me, for I believe the hunter must acknowledge his kill and his kill must know his hunter. Or hers, in your case."

He tapped the sword on the floor and seemed to trace something on it. As he did, his eyes fell to it, and I felt an intense pressure leave me. I squeezed my eyes shut, shook off the trance, and felt my legs loosen as I gained back a measure of control over my body. I opened one eye again to see him.

"I know you're a vampire." My voice faltered a little despite myself.

"True. But that is like me telling you you're human. It is, of course, what we are, but not *who* we are, yes?"

Ah, great, riddles.

I scrutinized him from head to toe. "I thought most vampires were all goth-wannabe-posers. Red sunglasses and leather jackets and too much gel in their hair. Aren't you a little old to cosplay as Edward?"

"You speak of popular culture. It is beneath both of us." He seemed to take a stance against the darkness with his sword and stabbed at it. "I am a creature of culture. I have not lived this long to abide by the rules of your petulant society without argument. Besides, I am far more than a vampire. I am an assassin. And I have caught my prey."

"Who, me?" Both eyes opened and stared at him. His spell over me was lessening, and I felt more of my old self coming back. Anger coursed through my veins at the gall of this dandily dressed 'assassin.' Yet, my legs still wouldn't move. He still had a power over me that kept me rooted to the spot, no matter how free my arms were. His spell was extraordinarily powerful, and an example of the power of a Varkolak over a normal vampire.

The vampires I had fought before were nearly senseless, dumb creatures, but they were nothing compared to this. In fact, Varkolaks had the power to create those kinds of vampires out of humans, although the *Pax Philosophia* explicitly banned the practice. Which I guessed explained why one would go into hiding and become an assassin.

"Yes, you. It was shockingly easy, too. All I had to do was endanger some innocent and you ran to the rescue like a good little puppet. I am disappointed it was so easy. I heard so many stories of you from the Fae and others. I expected a great battle of wits before a battle of arms, and here you stand before me, locked in place, dumb as a deer in headlights and as imminently dead."

"You sure talk a lot. Why don't you let my legs go and you can see if you're as good a fighter as you are an epic monologuer?" I dared.

"Hah," the vampire spat as his head fell back in mock laughter. "You challenge me?"

His face finally came into full view of the light, and I nearly retched. Something about his facial features was *wrong*. His eyes were a little too wide and far too sunken in, his nose a little too hooked. His lips were thin, and almost translucently white, and his gleaming teeth only accentuated how pale the rest of his skin was.

He looked slimy and gaunt. His hair was oily and pulled back tightly like it was running away from the horror show that was his face. Big, thick, bushy eyebrows bore down like they were attempting to menace me all on their own. Hundreds, perhaps thousands of years of passive malice wore on his forehead, etching wrinkles across his oily, pale skin.

"To a fair fight? Sure," I bluffed.

"I've always enjoyed playing with my food."

Suddenly, a large brown blur passed me. Before I knew what was happening, Dog knocked him down and was on top of him while barking loudly. As the vampire hit the floor, my legs released, and I nearly fell over when they suddenly had to handle holding my weight again. I stumbled forward a step or two and turned to the hurt fairy. Our eyes met.

"Go, go, go," I whispered, and he scrambled to his knees and crawled away.

I looked for the switchblade and saw it off to the side. It was far enough away the Varkolak would definitely notice me going for it, but I had to give it a shot. I ran and slid like a baseball player going hard into second, then hopped up onto my feet as I grabbed the blade. A sudden thought occurred to me. In movies, a wooden stake through the heart would take care of these suckers, but did that work on actual vampires from The Far? I hadn't yet tried this course of action. I thought hard about it. I knew there was something else in the stories, but it wouldn't immediately come to mind.

Dog was tearing at the creature when suddenly, he yelped and flew across the room. The vampire assassin stood and brushed himself off, only a minor tear on his jacket as evidence anything happened at all. Looking back, I supposed a lycanthrope tearing at your veins didn't do a lot if there was nothing in them in the first place.

Dog landed hard on the floor and smashed into a shelving unit. He looked up at me, and I read the apology and pain in his eyes. I made to go after him but stopped when the sword suddenly pointed at my throat. He whimpered from his place on the floor. I knew he was hurt, but right now, I had something else to worry about. The vampire leaned back on his leg and twirled the end of his blade in a slow circle.

CHAPTER TWELVE

"A fair distraction, but ultimately useless," the vampire slithered, his voice now sliding away from the authority and poshness and into a more rage-filled tone. He was upset he hadn't seen Dog coming and that I broke his spell, and knowing what I knew now, I avoided looking in his eyes. His tone let me know he was quite unhappy with that development.

"All right, but now it's time for a real fight." I dove, tucking and rolling until I reached another shelf, where an open box of tools lay.

It had to have something I could use. I crashed into it and tools spilled out of the top and my hand grabbed for the first metal thing I could put my fingers around. I spun to face him while waving it.

It was a wrench.

"*En garde.*" He thrust his sword.

I rolled my eyes and batted it away as I stepped away from the shelf. I didn't know a lot about sword fighting, but I knew having your back to something while fencing probably wasn't the best strategic move. He thrust again and I jumped to avoid it, and he pierced a box of what appeared to be sidewalk salt. It spilled on the floor in what began as a trickle and quickly became an avalanche of white. If nothing else, I wouldn't slip on that part of the floor any time soon.

I circled him slowly while waiting for him to try again and tried to figure out what I could do to fight him off. He was obviously quite strong, and his sword thrust seemed impossibly fast, but there had to be something I could do. I glanced back at the knocked-over box of tools and saw another wrench, a hammer and a screwdriver. My choices were limited to blunt force trauma and stabbing with a Phillips head. I could probably put together any table in the world, though.

I moved before my eyes registered what was happening, and brought the wrench up to my heart, barely catching the tip of the blade and knocking it away. It sliced into my arm and spilled blood down it. I spun into him, brought the wrench down in a hard arc, and smacked him in the jaw. That seemed enough to hurt him, and I brought it up again. Before I knew what was going on, his hand wrapped around my throat and he shoved me back into the boxes of tools. I flew ten feet across the room like it was nothing, and I marveled at his strength.

Suddenly, he was in the air and diving at me. I rolled barely in time and grabbed the hammer as I did so. He landed beside me and I swung hard, smashing it into his kneecap. I felt it crack and crumble under the shot and a ray of hope filled me. If I could hurt him, I could beat him.

He might be super strong, and super-fast, but nobody could fight that well with no knees.

I pulled back again as he screamed in pain and tried to take another swing, but he kicked me and connected with my nose. I heard him fall to the ground and pull away, but I was too busy with stars exploding in my vision and the sudden warmth of blood running down my face to go after him. I tried to shake it off, and when I looked back up, he was attempting to stand again.

I pulled my blade. It might not kill him, but it could certainly help. I rolled and grabbed the blade in one movement and flung it in an arc. It flew straight through the air and pierced the assassin's hand. He dropped the sword in surprise and yanked the blade from his hand as he knelt in pain and tossed it aside.

The sword landed between the two of us as the switchblade clattered to a stop in front of me. I grabbed it and stood. The vampire scrambled to his feet as well, and I dove to kick his sword away as his hands reached the area. I spun and swept his good leg, and he crashed to the floor again.

"This can't be happening." He backed up in a seated position as I stood.

"Oh, but it is, you greasy bloodsucker." I walked toward him while waving the blade so it caught the light and gleamed. "I'll cut your head off and send it to the people who sent you after me in a nice pretty box—" I began.

The vampire assassin suddenly threw his hand out, and salt filled my vision. It stung my eyes, and I dropped to one knee as I desperately tried to wipe it away. Defeated and pissed, he hissed at me and stumbled to his feet. He half-ran and half-hobbled away on his good leg and disappeared into the darkness. I could barely make out his outline through one teary eye as he left. After a moment, I heard the loud banging sound of a heavy door shutting and breathed a sigh of relief.

"Who the hell are you?" gurgled the man behind me.

My vision cleared more as I turned, allowing me to see the bleeding around the fairy's neck had slowed considerably and he now leaned against the shelving unit, half-sitting up and half laying in a pool of darkening red.

His eyes were wide and his face was pale from blood loss, but he looked as scared of me as he should have been of the assassin. My eyes shifted further down and saw Dog, who was lying on his side. He huffed heavily, and I knew that while he was hurt, he was okay.

"Sara Slick. Resident whoop-ass. Who the hell was that?" I gave a somewhat flailing gesture in the direction the vampire retreated.

"I haven't the slightest clue! I showed up because I got a call, and suddenly I had barbed wire around my neck and was being thrown! Everything hurts and nothing makes sense..." he muttered.

"Ah, well, I can help a little there. That was a vampire assassin, and he apparently laid a trap for me using you as bait so he could kill me and stop me from hunting down a guy who might cause the end of the world. And now that I say that out loud, I realize I probably should have stopped with vampire assassin," I finished with a resigned exhale.

"Look, I don't know who you are." The man scooted back on his ass toward the entrance I came in. "I don't *care* who you are, I don't want to know anything about you. I only want you to leave."

"I came here for supplies. Archie said," I began.

"Archie? Archie sent *you*? Jesus. Look, I don't care, you can have anything you want, just get the hell away from me." The man waved me away almost frantically.

"I don't know how much anything costs." I looked around the warehouse shelves as if I were looking for a price tag. Farstuff dealers weren't known for great advertising or static prices.

"Don't worry about it. Get it and go," he insisted.

Part of me was fairly sure he would end up tallying what I took and bill Archie, but I *did* save his life, so he owed me some kind of discount, I would think. I grabbed the items on Archie's list and a couple of others that looked interesting and walked past him again.

I went to check on Dog, who was obviously in pain, and I realized I would have to carry him back. He whimpered when I touched him, and I figured he might have broken bones on top of the lacerations. Grabbing what I needed and could carry along with Dog, I knelt and picked him up.

As gently as I could, I slung him over one shoulder and headed for the door. The dealer was clearing out the desk and packing things up, apparently content to move somewhere else for the rest of his career. Silently, I hoped it would be a beach somewhere, and the next time Archie needed something, I could take a detour for some swimming too. Probably not, though.

I sighed, headed for the door, and walked out into the dying daylight outside.

CHAPTER THIRTEEN

Dog wasn't a delicate creature. He was big, awkwardly shaped, and covered in fur that didn't smell like he had recently indulged in an oatmeal bath or a body spritz. His injuries made it harder for me to carry him, and by the time I hauled him to Archie's RV, my arms were about done.

"I could use a little help here," I called.

Ally and Archie rushed to the door and looked out at me.

"Shit," Archie muttered.

"It's so nice to see you, too, honey," I snarked. "I'm back from my shopping trip."

They jumped out and helped me balance Dog's mass and manipulated him into the RV. We carefully lowered Dog to the floor, and I made sure his head was positioned comfortably on the pillow.

"He's good," Archie reassured us.

"Good." I whipped my head over to him. "What kind of a last round of 'Supermarket Sweep,' grind a pound of coffee, you're only allowed five turkeys, leave the fucking diapers alone bullshit was that?"

"What?" he asked.

"I thought I was going to do a little shopping. Weird, creepy-ass shopping, but shopping nonetheless. I had my list. I showed up at the scary building that seems to be the status quo for these people, all ready to meet up with your Farstuff dealer and get what we need. But did I find a nice man ready to sell me some dragons' teeth and cyclops eyelashes? No. I find a fairy getting hanged from the shelving with barbed wire by a freaking vampire. That was not delightful. Dog showed up and saved my ass but as you can see, he didn't fare too well." I let out a breath.

Ally and I gathered first aid supplies and started going over Dog's body, identifying each of his injuries so we could clean them and patch them up.

"A vampire?" Archie asked.

"Yeah. And not one of those Hot Topic Halloween Clearance sale dudes like in the basement that time. Nope. A Varkolak. This was a nasty creature who had way too much fun stringing the guy up. I'm tired of innocent people being used as bait to lure me out," I pointed out.

"Well," Archie shrugged slightly and rocked his head back and forth. "That's kind of up for interpretation. Remember, he's a Farstuff dealer. His hands aren't totally clean. Take heart in knowing he wasn't a completely innocent person."

"He's not dead," I informed him.

"Oh. Well, that's a bonus. Still. Not totally innocent." He gestured with one hand like he was drawing a line at that evaluation.

"Has he ever specifically done something against me?"

"Not that I know of." Archie adjusted one of the bandages I put into place like he had the compulsion to do something.

"Did he feed information about me to Hobbes?"

"I doubt it." He shook his head.

"Did he have a former life as an Agent of the Guild and was one of the masked guys who arrested me ten years ago?" I smoothed another bandage in place and paused to look at Archie.

"That seems extraordinarily unlikely," he admitted.

"Right. We'll stick with innocent," I concluded.

Archie nodded, then something seemed to dawn on him. "A Varkolak? Are you sure? I thought they were all dead."

"What's a Varkolak?" Ally asked from behind him as she examined Dog's injuries, suddenly paying attention to our conversation again.

"An ancient vampire, but more than that," Archie explained. "They're born, not made. They're extremely rare now—I thought they were all dead—but there are stories of them nearly ruling The Far eons ago. They can turn humans into little worker-vampires, which is what Slick has run into before. Varkolaks are exceptionally powerful, very strong and intelligent. No offense, but I'm a little surprised you made it back."

"Thanks for the vote of confidence in my skills, Archie."

His eyes swept over the bag still hanging from my shoulder. "Let me see what you got."

I took the bag off my shoulder and handed it to him. Dog writhed in pain as we pressed a piece of gauze to a cut in his side to stop the bleeding. I looked down at him and cringed. I hated to see him going through this. The only reason he faced any of that was because he tried to help me. Beside me, Archie unpacked the bag and spread everything I picked out across one of his large tables. I heard him making sounds as he went through everything. Eventually, I turned to him.

"Something you want to share with the class?"

He looked up from one of the jars I brought and shook his head. "None of this is good quality."

I let out an exasperated sound. "Seriously? I went through all that, and you're criticizing the quality of what I brought back to you?"

"It's not you. I mean, you're the one who brought the stuff back, but you got what you could. The dealer isn't supplying good materials. I'll have to remember that the next time my stash runs low. It's..." He picked up a few of the items and looked at them in disgust.

"It's what?"

The RV's floor squeaked, and I looked up to see Pip walking up from the back while nibbling her way through a large roll in one hand and gripping what looked like a slice of pizza in the other. Her eyes fell on Dog and widened.

"What is that?" she asked.

"This is Dog," Ally told her. "He had a rough day."

"It's what, Archie?" I prodded him to continue.

"We barely have a plan as it is, and only having access to low-quality supplies won't help. And now we have a freaking vampire assassin on our tail. Things don't look great for us right now." He put everything back in the bag and set it down.

"I don't understand. Slick told me vampires are all punks, and she whupped this one's ass already. What are you so worried about?" Ally sounded confused.

"I didn't say they were punks," I argued.

"You said they were mall goth wannabes," she insisted.

"I might have said that," I agreed.

"Vampires are one of those creatures people gravely misunderstand. Real vampires, the Varkolaks, are extremely rare. Most of them are ancient. You won't find any of them sparkling or making women go weak in the knees with their dashing good looks. These creatures are ugly. They have large jaws, chilling eyes, and long, thin arms and legs." Archie waved his arms around like he should be standing at the edge of a used car lot.

"Oh, so we're dealing with Slenderman," Ally said.

"Who's Slenderman?" I asked.

She shook her head and brushed me away. "I'll tell you later."

"These things are no legend, and you'll never mistake them for something that might be kind and nurturing. Real vampires are fast, strong, and bloodthirsty. They don't have any of the classic vampire weaknesses like people think." Archie looked completely serious about what he was saying.

"So, the garlic necklaces I planned won't do any good?" I asked.

Pip had made her way over to the cot and knelt beside it. Now she lightly stroked Dog's fur, and although I would have thought that would aggravate him, it seemed to calm him down.

"Garlic doesn't do anything to them. There's no point in looking specifically for an ash tree to get wood for a stake. They can walk around out in the sunlight with abandon. None of those things will hurt them." Archie shook his head. "But they can die like anything else."

"If they can die, what's the big deal?" I asked.

"They're vicious when they want to destroy someone or are looking for blood. They can also enchant humans, which brings them under their control and gives them trace amounts of power. That's the weakling vampires most people encounter. They tend to be more dramatic and unpredictable, but they're nothing compared to their creators. They aren't very powerful, but creating them is considered a breach of the *Pax Philosophia*, so it doesn't happen very often."

"Lovely," I muttered.

"Not exactly. Real vampires aren't something you want to mess with. We're screwed if one is after us. Getting hunted down isn't something I relish," Archie commented.

"I can't imagine why." I glared at him through narrowed eyes. "It's so much fun to have people wanting you dead and going to extreme measures to find you and wipe you out." I looked at Dog, who finally seemed to be calming down after Ally gave him a large dose of medicine from Archie's cabinet. "Look, vampire or no vampire, things haven't changed. The plan is the same. We still need to go. But we can't leave Dog here."

"What?" Archie asked. "You want to bring that thing along?"

"I'm not abandoning him. Especially after what he went through. He's coming with us," I insisted.

"Now we get a dog, too?" Pip said excitedly.

"I mean, it's not quite like that," I began.

Dog barked out a somewhat happy sound, and Pip giggled while stroking his fur.

"Fine." I sighed, then added, "But you're responsible for taking him on walks."

"Pip, your face is sliding off," I whispered out of the corner of my mouth

She looked at me and did her best to adjust the mask stretched awkwardly over her lizard features. Her enthusiastic changes resulted in cockeyed eyeholes and the mouth positioned somewhere in the vicinity of her chin.

"Better?" she asked.

I looked her up and down, taking in the disguise we hastily put together. A trench coat tied at the waist made a makeshift dress and a massive floppy hat did its best to conceal her head and the awkward mask. She shuffled along in a pair of patent leather flats, the only type of shoes we could find that fit her unusually shaped feet. I turned to Archie.

"Are you positive there's nothing you could do to make the rune work better?" I asked Archie.

"She looks like every other Londoner I've ever seen," he said plainly. I stared at him until he wilted and sighed.

He had put together a quick rune that now hung

around Pip's neck. It was designed to make her appear more human, but the effect was somewhat short of convincing. Especially since it did absolutely nothing for her tail. Instead, we had to duct tape her tail to one leg, resulting in a strange gait somewhere between a waddle and a scoot.

"That's the best I could do with such short notice. Stop paying so much attention to her. If she acts completely normal and like she's supposed to be here, people won't pay as much attention to her. They won't want to stare at her or make any comments for fear of being labeled insensitive. Sometimes political correctness really does work out for us," he announced like he was an authority on the subject. With his pointy ears, he might be.

I tightened my hands around the strap of my carry-on bag and looked around the airport nervously.

"Do you think we got here with enough time?" I asked.

"Our flight doesn't leave for another three hours," Ally pointed out.

"And it said for international travel you should arrive at the airport at least three hours before take-off. At least. That means more than three hours. And we only have three hours." I pointed at the clock on the wall to under-score my point.

"Slick, it will be fine. I promise," she reassured me.

It was my first time on a plane, so the entire process was foreign to me. Fortunately, it seemed Archie chose a flight at a quieter time at the airport because there were only a handful of other people making their way through the terminal with us. Of those, most of them had spent an unmistakable amount of time staring at my group as we passed by.

Some of them focused on the inhuman human that was Pip, while others focused directly on Archie's shoulders. That was where we were keeping Dog for the time being. Drugging him up at the lab ensured he wouldn't be in pain during the travel, but it also knocked him for a loop, and he was pretty much not good for anything at that point.

Everyone who stared at him looked terrified, which I assumed was not the reaction most emotional support animals received. He would have to work on being more convincing. He was far too big to stuff into a carrier and put under the seat, which meant he was now officially on the job supporting me emotionally.

I definitely needed it. The closer we got to security, the more nervous I became. Flying was one of those life experiences I always expected I'd have after graduating high school. Maybe I'd go on some grand adventure to celebrate or when I got into college, could participate in an exchange program. I didn't know who would want to exchange me or for what, but it would probably involve a plane ride.

As we all know, that's not how it worked out for me. Now I was staring down the barrel of my first flight, and it would be a doozy. This wasn't a little puddle hop to the next state or even a cross-country jaunt. This was an international journey. We were in it for the long haul.

But speaking of barrels.

"Do you think Splinter is doing all right?" I asked Archie.

He glanced at his shoulder to where the massive dog's head lolled around.

"Still stuffed in the barrel and wrapped up in a bandage," he told me. "He's probably as comfortable as the rest of us will be on this trip."

Since we doubted any of us could pull off having an unidentifiable rodent creature as an additional emotional support animal, we concealed Splinter for the journey. After taking a cue from the massive fluffy rescue dogs who bounded through the snow to save stranded people, we stuffed him into a small barrel and latched it around Dog's neck. If anyone asked, we would tell them it was supplies for his duties as my dog.

We finally got to security, and I was relieved to see there was no one else there. This would go so much smoother than I thought.

Which was the exact thought that should have told me it would be a disaster.

"No," Archie said a few minutes later while standing in front of a security agent. "Flying Batwing Newt eyeballs isn't a euphemism for anything."

"You need to go over to the next table and unpack your bag," the unamused man told him.

"Pip, pip, cheerio," Archie sang as he swept his bag off the first counter and carried it over to the second.

"Me?" Pip asked. "Does he need something?"

"Not you," I told her. "Archie has lost touch with all language ability."

"I don't know about you, kind sir, but I most frequently use my tincture of dissolved troll skin to deal with puncture wounds," Archie spat. "And *that* is a slinky."

I shook my head and looked away from Archie. The angry-looking guard in front of me glared at Dog in my arms. Because our tickets listed him as my emotional support animal, security told Archie he wasn't permitted to bring him through the checks. That meant I had to haul him around along with my luggage.

"Do you have any weapons or other dangerous objects on you?" the agent asked me.

"A serape is the perfect versatile clothing piece in case I get a little chilly. The telescoping spoon, I feel, is self-explanatory. Might I say, you have lovely irises in your eyeballs." Archie continued his attempt at being human.

I shook my head and tried to focus on what my agent was asking me.

"I'm sorry. What?" I looked back at the agent.

"Do you have any weapons or other dangerous objects on you?" he repeated.

My mouth went dry, but I reminded myself that Archie had prepared me for this. The penny dipped in pixie tears that was actually a tiny rune sitting in my pocket would stop them from identifying my switchblade and the runes Archie armed me with. But that didn't stop me from worrying they'd catch it. I drew a breath and lugged Dog through the metal detector.

"What if a leak springs up? How exactly do you expect me to effectively deal with a situation like that without duct tape? I think six rolls is conservative," Archie exclaimed.

"Okay, Archie, I know you're having a good time talking with this charming gentleman, but he needs to do his job, and we have a plane to catch. Why don't you pack every-thing back into your bag so we can get going?" Ally interceded.

Like always, her charm won out. She managed to sweet-talk Archie out of the grasp of the increasingly suspicious TSA agent. Just like she convinced them not to stare too hard at her "little sister" who was recovering from several reconstructive surgeries and this was her first venture out into public.

"I've never seen an emotional support dog someone has to carry through security," one of the agents said. The derisive tone in his voice was impossible to miss.

"This is how he supports me emotionally," I snapped back.

"How is that?" he needled.

"Taking care of him requires all my focus, so I'm not able to concentrate on the things around me that may lead to anxiety. He gives me a sense of accomplishment and confidence that keeps me even and prevents emotional meltdowns." I was talking right out of my ass, but they seemed to buy it.

"You definitely don't want to see her without him," Archie added. "Her having an anxiety attack is..." he gestured like his head was exploding, "it's bad."

"Yep, so it's better for everyone involved if he keeps on with his highly trained behaviors," I told them.

Ally rushed us the rest of the way through the security area and to the gate. She dropped into one of the hard plastic chairs and glared at us.

"Are you trying to get added to the no-fly list before you get on a plane? Archie, why the hell did you need a single flip-flop in your luggage?" she asked.

He glared at her. "I have my reasons."

She sighed. "And have you never spoken to a human before? Before me, anyway?"

He gave a half-shrug, unable to deny it. "I'm not good at it."

Two hours later, I sat in my seat while gripping Dog in my lap. A sleep mask acted as my blindfold, and I chewed gum like it was my job.

"Slick?" Ally said from beside me as she lifted my sleep mask away from my eyes. "The little kid across the aisle looks pretty terrified of Dog."

"I don't care. He's here to emotionally support me." I lifted my chin defiantly.

"No, he's not," she pointed out.

"Shhhh." I widened my eyes and shook my head.

The plane started rolling, and I gripped Dog harder. He gave a wimpy half-growl through his drug-induced stupor, and a flight attendant took a cautious step toward us. The warning from the pilot for all crew to take their seats averted disaster. I dropped my head back against the seat and Ally readjusted my mask. The plane got faster and faster, and the anxiety grew until I felt the ground disappear beneath us. We made it. Barely, but we made it. Now we only had to survive the flight.

CHAPTER FIFTEEN

"Who did you say this apartment belongs to?" I asked.

"Flat," Ally corrected. "We're in London, so it's called a flat."

"For something called a flat, it sure seems pretty damn vertical to me." I let out a distinctly unfeminine grunt as I hauled my luggage up another of the narrow steps leading up through the building.

"We're almost there," she told me. "I stayed here one time while on assignment."

"I thought you worked for an online magazine. I didn't think they would send you all the way to London for a project," I said.

"It was a one-time thing. I took someone else's place when they got sick right before the trip. It's a cute place. Kind of cozy for this many people, but we'll make it work." She dragged her bag up another step.

"As long as there are no bones or dissolved corpses, and I have enough room for my lungs to expand with a full breath, I'm good," I told her.

"I really wish I could think you were joking about that," Ally pointed out. "However, in light of recent events, I think I've lost that luxury."

"Well," I made it up another two steps before taking a break, "you still didn't answer my question."

"It belongs to a colleague named Phillip."

"Oooh, Phillip," I teased. Her eyes flickered over to Archie and guilt I didn't really know if I should feel squeezed my heart. "Sorry. It's still a compulsion that comes out now and then."

"It's fine. Phillip is definitely not an oooh. He's…Phillip. But it was nice of him to let us stay here." She looked straight ahead like she hoped if she didn't discuss the comment any more, it would go away.

"Why did he? I mean, what did you tell him?" Archie asked.

A slight edge to his voice suggested maybe that flicker of guilt was justified.

"I told him I would be here in London for an important assignment and could use a place to crash for a few days," Ally said.

"Did he suggest he come, too?" Archie asked.

She looked at him as we finally made it all the way to the door of the flat.

"Absolutely. He told me to be waiting in a bathtub of tea and he'd bring the crumpets." Ally slung her bag to the foot of the door.

"I don't know what that means," I said.

Ally rolled her eyes and unlocked the door. We dragged ourselves, our bags, and Dog inside and dropped every-thing, save Dog, on the floor. He ended up draped across a plaid sofa that had enough off-beat personality to make the rest of the surroundings even cooler.

"All right. Let's freshen up and head out," I suggested.

Ally groaned. "Can't we sleep for a little while? That was a million-hour flight."

"And if you had worn a sleep mask and earplugs like I told you to, you would have slept perfectly well through most of it," I pointed out.

"You only slept that well because Dog was crushing you and you had limited air supply." She dropped onto a couch.

"Well, it worked out swimmingly. Come on, we really should get moving. Let's go over the plan one more time. Senator Cabot is staying at the Crepe," I started.

"The Egg," Ally corrected.

"Damn it. I knew it was a breakfast food." I shook my head.

"It's also called the Gherkin." She took her hair out of its ponytail and casually ran her fingers through the dark strands.

I blinked at her a few times. "Like the tiny pickle?"

"That's not actually its name. It's simply what people call it," she pointed out.

"Oh, my God." I rubbed my temples. "It doesn't matter. It's the big pointy one."

"That looks like a Faberge Egg," she said.

"Oh. Now that makes sense. Anyway. Cabot is staying in one of the residences that's been converted into a VIP hotel suite. We'll play the room service gambit." I pointed at her. "Ally, you'll be our decoy. You'll dress up as the hotel waitress and move around the hallways, undetected."

"And you will also be undetected because you will be in the food cart," she continued.

"Yes. Then, once we're in, we'll find a way to convince the powerful world leader she is in danger and needs to trust us—complete strangers with no political ties or law enforcement clearance. Should be fine." I flashed a double thumbs-up.

"It will be," Archie concurred. "It will go exactly like we planned it out. And if it doesn't, we deal with it at that point."

"Do you have anything for me? Fancy weapons? Cool new gadgets? Paper that will automatically convince anyone who looks at it I have authorization to be there and should be trusted?" I asked.

"I'm still not Doctor Who, but I started watching and I think I can rip off some of his little playthings." Archie nodded optimistically.

"Oh, snap. I totally forgot you watched that show," Ally laughed. "You were such a nerd."

"I was not a nerd! It was compelling storytelling set against a rich tapestry of science-fiction and urban fantasy," I defended.

"Uh-huh. Like those are ever words you would care about using." She shook her head, and another laugh bubbled up.

"I'm thinking about going back to the very beginning of the series. I just got through the eleventh Doctor, and I feel like I might not fully appreciate the story because I don't know the other iterations of him." Archie stared into the distance thoughtfully.

"Tenth Doctor," I corrected. "There are ten."

"Actually, they're on number thirteen now," he told me.

"What?" I snapped.

"Ok, before she storms Cardiff and demands restitution, we should go ahead with the plan," Archie announced. "I don't have any fancy new things for you right now, but I'll start working on some. Hopefully, you won't need any weapons or special gadgets during this phase. Your goal is simply to warn Cabot and get her out of danger."

"All right, let's go," Pip declared enthusiastically.

"Not this time," Archie told her. "You need to stay here."

"But I want to go," the young Lizard Person protested.

"No. We don't know what will happen out there. Besides, we need you to stay here and look after Dog." I gestured at the couch. "Speaking of which."

I reached over to where Dog lay and released the hatch on the barrel around his neck. A bundle of bandages tumbled out and unraveled to reveal Splinter. He lay still for a few seconds while blinking his beady little eyes as he processed what happened, then got up and ran for the kitchen. I had to hand it to him. He had a nose for food.

I grabbed a handful of cereal from a box I found in a cabinet and made a little pile for him. He stuffed a bunch in his cheeks and I funneled the rest into my pocket for him.

"Are you sure I can't come? I would probably fit in the food cart better." Pip curled up to demonstrate her ability to become compact.

"You probably would. But we don't want to put you in any danger." I smiled at her, wanting to convince her so we could move on sooner. "Hang out here. If our previous missions are any indication, there will be plenty of excitement to go around."

My head smashed against the top of the food cart, and my knee bashed up into my chin.

"Ow! What the hell are you doing out there, Ally? Rolling me up and down the stairs?" I hissed.

"Shh," Ally shushed sharply. "Keep it down. People will hear you."

I went silent for a few seconds, then chuckled. "You know, it sure was easy for you to talk your way right into the hotel."

"Is that some sort of veiled ethnic reference?" she asked.

"I'm not sure how it would be," I pointed out. "Especially since this isn't a hotel, as you reminded me three times on the way over here. I meant you're too freaking good at this spy stuff."

"It's my calling. Besides, one of the team has to be a people person, considering everyone who meets you wants to punch you. Now, shut up." She pushed the cart a little faster as if to make up for the conversation.

We rolled along for another few minutes. After a strangely disorienting elevator ride, we rolled up to a door. I could see shoes from under the bottom edge of the white cloth covering the food cart. It seemed several security guards were posted outside Cabot's door. That put a bit of a chink in the plan.

"Hello, gentleman. If you'll excuse me," Ally said.

She took a slight step toward the door, but they didn't shift and she stopped.

"No one goes into the Senator's room," one guard informed her.

"Absolutely. I'm so glad to hear she's well-protected during her visit here. I do need to slip in really fast. In and out." Again she tried to take a step, but these men seemed immune to her sweet talk.

"No one goes into the Senator's room," the guard repeated.

"I'm room service. I want to deliver her order to her," Ally insisted.

"Senator Cabot didn't order anything from room service. There must be a mistake." His voice was getting more aggravated rather than more charmed.

Shit.

"It's no mistake. I don't make mistakes. I'm very good at my job. Actually, I'm very, very good at many things," she purred.

I rolled my eyes and withheld a gag.

"Get lost before we alert the hotel." The security guard was obviously not impressed.

The cart immediately started rolling.

"Have a nice day, gentlemen," she snipped.

We rolled for a few minutes, then I heard the heavy thud of a door closing and assumed she brought me into a stairwell.

"What now? They won't let us in the room," Ally said.

"Now, we try for Plan B."

CHAPTER SIXTEEN

"What the fuck are you doing, Slick?" I muttered to myself.

"You can't be serious," Ally said. "You really can't be serious."

"What kind of shit did you get yourself into?" I asked myself.

I wrapped the firehose around my waist another time and tied it as tightly as I could. It didn't feel terribly secure, but that was firehoses for you. Not the best in fashion or personal security devices.

"This is a bad idea," Ally said.

I shrugged and flashed her a smile. "I know. But remember, you're the one who's good at charming and sweet-talking. I'm good at bad ideas." I strode over to the side of the building and peered over the edge. Just as quickly, I snapped back and squeezed my eyes shut. "Oh, holy jeebus."

"You look like you need your emotional support animal," Ally quipped.

"I need my emotional support cherry picker and

harness. That is really freaking high." I took another look at Ally. She looked terrified. "Don't worry. It'll be fine. Look, I don't even have any helicopters shooting at me or trying to blow me up. I'm already way ahead of the game. It'll be all right. Trust me. Besides, Splinter is back at the flat and is scared of heights. He'd only throw up on me and make my hands slippery."

"Lovely imagery. I trust you. I don't trust the fact that this plan is based on a stupid movie from the '90s."

"Hey," I shouted. *Die Hard* is from the late '80s. And it's a classic."

I gave my best friend a reassuring smile, tugged on the firehose one more time roller coaster belt-style, and climbed onto the edge of the roof. London from above was beautiful, a glittering jewel of lights and sounds. Also, impending death from falling, but no city was immune to that when you stood on the side of a tall building. A gust of wind hit me in the face and I swayed backward, then gripped the stone as hard as I could. Ally gasped.

"Slick, seriously. Get down. There has to be some other way we can do this."

"We already tried the other way. Those security guards won't let anything past them. There's no way we'll get into Cabot's room if you expect to stroll through the door." I closed my eyes and drew in a steeling breath.

"I didn't expect to stroll. I expected to walk in with a respectful and dignified gait." She swept her hand in front of her to demonstrate how regal she could be.

"The point is, you could stroll, you could stride, you could rhumba. They won't let you through. We figured out which window is hers. All I have to do is get through it, and I'll be in. Don't worry. Be ready when I call you. It'll be fine. I got this," I reassured her.

Another gust of wind blew up as I adjusted my position on the edge of the roof. The plan was to ease my way down the side of the building until I came to Cabot's window and get inside. I had absolutely no intention of leaping or swinging around down there. Unfortunately, there's a reason they call them intentions and not blueprints. I was getting into the position to step down off the edge of the roof when an even more intense wind knocked me off balance.

Ally cried out as I toppled off the building and started sliding down the front of it.

"I don't got this," I called up to her.

I held tighter to the firehose and swung my legs forward to plant my boots against the side of the building. The thick rubber soles created traction, and I pressed as hard as I could until I regained control of my movement. Moving them made me spin around, and I caught myself again.

"Are you okay?" Ally called from the roof.

"I got it. Back under control." I looked up and realized she wasn't standing at the edge, looking down at me. "Are you seriously not going to come check on me?"

"Absolutely not. Unless you want my ass tumbling right down after you, it's staying exactly where it is." She sounded even farther away.

"All right, I'm headed down." I stopped myself from committing the grave mistake of looking down again.

The wind was more intense here than it had been on the roof. Either that, or I felt each breeze a little more clearly now that I was dangling out in the open. I gripped the fire hose with both hands as I planted my feet and started working my way down the building. I couldn't believe I was doing this. This was definitely not in my "what I want to be when I grow up" report from my last year in high school.

I concentrated as hard as I could on rappelling down the building. I didn't get the chance to measure the distance from the roof to Cabot's window or the length of the fire hose. I could only hope it was enough to get me there, but not so much that it would be hard to stop. The wind got stronger, and my boots slipped against the glass. My stomach clenched, and I tightened my jaw to help me concentrate. My feet slipped again, and it felt like gravity took hold of me and tried to yank me down.

This equipment definitely wasn't right for the job, but it was what I had and I wasn't going to turn my back on it. After a few seconds, I grew more confident and sped up as I moved down the side of the building. A little hop against the side that brought me down a couple of feet gave me a boost of confidence, but soon, I hopped too hard and the wind grabbed me before I made it back to the glass.

I twirled around at the end of the fire hose while struggling to get back to the building. Above me, the length of hose kept unreeling from its metal wheel, and I could only imagine it coming loose and me gliding down the side of the building like an ice luge gone terribly wrong.

I finally fought my way back under control. Pure grit kept me in place as I made my way down to the next window. I wondered how many people were watching me and how many times I had ended up splashed across various social media accounts. It really didn't matter. As long as it didn't interfere with me, they could gather around and gawk.

I quickly realized I was only talking a big game. I sincerely hoped there weren't people down below watching and recording every move I made. Finally, I counted the right number of windows and realized I was almost there. I prepared myself, then reached into my pocket and pulled out my switchblade.

I doubted Solon ever pictured me using it for something like this.

He would be proud of me right now. I told myself to stay calm. After moving down the short distance to bring me right to the window, I looked at the tool in my hand. It was nothing short of perfect. The creation behind it was masterful, and I had gotten familiar and comfortable with using it in various different ways. There was no way a normal switchblade would do what I needed, but nothing about Solon was normal.

For that matter, nothing about me was normal.

I brought myself up against the window and let myself down a few more inches until I was in front of the right space. Then I unfolded the switchblade, touched the tip of the blade to the glass, and drew a breath. The switchblade cut through the glass like it was silk, and with a triumphant feeling in my chest, I pulled myself inside.

The interior of the building was impossibly dark. I quickly detached myself from the firehose and let it drop down the building. I heard something deeper in the apartment and followed it. The farther I went inside, the more obvious it became that the sound I heard was snoring. I let it guide me until I found the bedroom and carefully let myself inside.

The woman in the bed was Senator Cabot. I had seen her many times on the news and in print. I couldn't mistake her. I watched her for a few seconds, feeling guilty for interfering with her quiet moments. Knowing I couldn't wait any longer or more danger would come, I crept over to the side of the bed and placed my hand over her mouth. With my free hand, I reached over to the night-stand and flipped the switch on the lamp to turn the light on.

I leaned as close as I could while trying to find the line of being creepy and hoping I didn't cross it. "Don't scream. I'm here to help you."

CHAPTER SEVENTEEN

"Who the hell are you?" she whispered loudly at me as I held my finger to my mouth again. She might be a world leader and a brilliant politician, but she seemed to have a hard time grasping the whole 'be quiet' thing.

Although to be fair, I did break through her window near the top of a famous giant building and got past what was assuredly a well-paid and highly trained security staff to do it, so perhaps she was right to be rather surprised.

"Name's Sara Slick. I promise I'm not here to murder you." I offered her as much of a smile as I could.

This seemed to not have the calming effect I intended. Instead, her eyes went wide with panic and she seemed to back up on the bed, crawling away from me. I held out my hands to show there were no weapons, nor did I pose a threat.

"Get away from me," she whispered again, then drew in a deep breath, no doubt to call the highly trained, very serious guards I had thus far avoided.

"Wait! Let me tell you who I am," I whisper-yelled, and

she stopped. For a moment, the panic and fear seemed to fall away in favor of curiosity. If I could hold her attention long enough, I might have a shot at avoiding going through the window the hard way. Or back to The Deep.

"So, you're telling me you're from another dimension?" She squinted with her head cocked to one side so her overall impression was not unlike a confused cocker-spaniel.

"Not exactly, no." I shook my head. "But I've been there, and trust me, that place is bonkers. In the worst way. And forces from that side are out to get you. I've been doing this dance with bad guys from that side for a long time now, and trust me, you and your guards are *not* prepared for what they have at their disposal. These are some of the most vile, vicious, and magically inclined creatures any universe in any dimension has ever seen. They're nasty and ruthless and will hunt you down until your last breath. I've avoided being dead by the absolute skin of my teeth and I *know* about them."

"Ok, so what if I believe you? What can you do to help me?"

There was a mocking tone in her voice I didn't much care for, but I understood it. This was a person who was almost sure I was a looney tune nut job who managed to get by her soon-to-be-fired security and was now conspiracy theory dumping at her in the middle of the night when she had important political bullshit to do tomorrow.

If I was her, I might think the same thing. Yet there was

a small part of that voice, and through the words she chose, that told me I was getting somewhere. Maybe not fast enough, but I was getting there.

"Well, the first thing we need to do is get you the hell out of here. For one, you literally could not have picked a more conspicuous place to stay." I gestured around us like I was encompassing the entire building. "This thing is a giant glittery beacon of wealth and power, and you're staying in a secret room only given to super-secret special people? That means there's fewer people who know when it's been breached, and fewer people to eliminate when they decide to interfere. Beside all that, if I could find you, they can. I didn't even try very hard. They have unlimited money to bribe people and spies in every imaginable level of government you can think of. These guys are everywhere and if they want you, they can usually get to you. You're damn lucky I got here when I did."

"But where would we go?" she asked.

"Well, I haven't worked that part out yet, not all the way." I pointed back through the window. "I have some friends who can help us, and if we can get you to them, we'll find a place that's secure for you and keep you safe until we can figure out what comes next."

"And you're sure these people are coming after me? That you can help me?" She stared at me like she was right on the edge of believing me and was waiting for me to push her over.

I nodded. "I am surer of both of those things than anything else in the world. You're in danger. I can help."

"Let me pack a bag." She threw the blanket off her and stood. Part of me went on high alert, thinking she would make a break for the hotel room door and call for the guards, but she didn't. She reached into her suitcase, which stood open on the couch on the wall, grabbed a few items from it, and tossed them into a designer handbag. As she debated between two articles of clothing, I looked around the room.

So, this was how the rich stayed? Not bad. Not quite my run-down, no electricity, no hot water flophouse back home, but pretty good. Certainly better than the mobile battle station that was Archie's RV. From my vantage point, I could see into the little kitchenette area where a tray of cookies and fruit sat to welcome the guest. A bottle of wine sat behind that, and while I was never a wine person per se, nicking that and bringing it back might make the flat a little less stressful for everyone involved. There was a sitting area by the door with couches and a large TV, and a desk where a laptop sat, open but off in the corner.

It was a posh room, with all the little gold fixtures and fancy lighting and comfortable seating, but still a hotel room. After a while they all seemed the same, no matter how spruced up they were. My eyes drifted to the bathroom across from me and the fancy towels on the sink. They were white and fluffy and probably smelled like fresh cotton, and I wondered how terribly inappropriate it would be for me to break back into the room once we got her safe and take a bath just so I could use those towels.

Something bright glinted in the light and caught my eye. I stared at my reflection in the mirror while trying to place what it was that seemed so odd. On the other side of the room, Cabot was talking to me, but I wasn't really paying much attention. I'd found what it was that struck me so oddly. It was under her pillow, a small part of it sticking out and shining in the light. Very slowly, I turned around and looked at the pillow. I couldn't see it from my vantage point, but if I lifted it...

It was a knife. A really nice knife. A really nice, *long* knife. With elaborately carved hieroglyphs on it. A really nice, long, hieroglyph-covered and *glowing* knife. Clearly, this was magic-infused. Why the hell did Cabot have a magic-infused knife?

The world felt like it lost all of its color and oxygen all at once. My chest crushed inside of me and it felt like the inside of my skull was suddenly full of cotton balls. My face tingled and my eyes watered at the edges as the thoughts collided in my skull. Something else was different in the room.

Cabot was no longer talking.

I turned to her, and to me it felt like it took years to go from facing the pillow to facing her, but the time distillation evaporated with the springing sound of the taser she shot at me. The wires with the tiny, sharp prongs on the end flew out and caught me right in the chest. Electricity flowed through them before they caught enough of my skin to dig in, and a scream caught in my throat as everything went white.

I felt myself convulse on the floor of the hotel room, but it was as if my brain had paused. I couldn't think or feel anything other than pain. Then it was over. The prongs were still in me, but the shock had ceased, and I breathed out heavily, a whimper coming out despite myself. I tried to put my hands under me and push myself up, but two hands were already under my arms and yanking me to my feet.

Two burly security guards hauled me up and toward the door where Cabot stood, taser gun in her hand. One of the guards pulled something from his jacket and shook it open. It was a black bag. As he flung it up and yanked it down, and it went over my head blocking out my vision, the last thing I saw was Cabot standing at the door with a large, weird, and terribly satisfied smile on her face. I made a sound and the electric volts wound through me again, and in the darkness of the hood, I passed out.

CHAPTER EIGHTEEN

I woke to the sounds of a chair scraping across the floor. Everything was dark, and I smelled canvas all around me. My head felt like someone was driving a railroad spike directly in the center of my skull, and I tasted blood in the back of my mouth. So, you know, normal Wednesday in the life of Sara Slick. Things started coming together slowly, and it dawned on me what happened before I went lights out and woke up tasting my plasma.

That bitch.

Cabot played me so well. But what was the deal with the knife? Was she one of them? Or did she happen to have a rune-filled, super-nice, big-ass knife under her pillow in case intruders popped in on her on the millionth floor of a building? Which, to be fair, I did, so maybe point taken, but why the Far knife? As I wondered how she got it and what it meant that she had it, the world exploded in light.

Everything was washed out for a moment, a sea of brilliant white so bright I had to shut my eyes, then color and shapes began to fade in from the outside and work their way in. I was barely able to make out the shapes of the two big guards who grabbed me back at the room when a fist appeared in my cleared vision and immediately knocked it back out for a moment.

My head rocked back as the fist connected with my jaw, then snapped forward until my chin rested on my chest. I wanted to respond by whipping the ever-loving hell out of the owner of that fist, but my hands went nowhere. They were zip-tied to the chair. I struggled momentarily against them, more out of hope they were as bad at restraining people as they were at keeping rooftop intruders out. No such luck.

"Talk," the owner of the fist said in the matter-of-fact tone every dumb thug thinks is the way to get someone under duress to confess to whatever it is they want them to confess to.

"I was born on a farm in upstate Kissmyass," I told him. A hard punch to the gut ended my retort.

"Either you tell us what we want to know, or I keep hitting." Another punch underscored the threat.

He was thick and so white he was almost translucent. His haircut screamed he murdered puppies for fun and made sure all his shoes faced west at night to keep the brain goblins away. Haircut would be his name as far as I was concerned, and his partner, another thick-bodied simpleton with a military cut and thick-rimmed glasses would be Four-Eyes.

"You're pretty. You were always pretty. Don't listen to what all the other boys say. They like you, that's why they tease." I stared at him without cringing.

Another really solid crunch into my ribs, and I couldn't

breathe for a moment. As I wheezed, Four-Eyes put his hand on Haircut's chest and moved him away. Apparently, he was going to play Good Cop today. I nearly threw up. Whether that was because of the repeated body blows or the boredom of their terrible interrogation technique, I couldn't be sure.

I tried to look around the room while they quietly pretended to argue about tactics and Four-Eyes twirled the chair around so he could sit on it backward. It was like watching one of those cop dramas on rerun for the thousandth time. I could almost write his dialogue for him, he was so predictable.

The room was dark and dank, with one bright, naked light bulb above us. I wasn't sitting behind a table, so that cliché of cop shows was missing, but I was zip-tied to a folding chair that creaked when I moved and there was a hole in the upper part of the wall that had bars on it so I could see a dark blue sky with stars. I figured we were in some kind of black site and the room's surroundings were designed to intimidate the prisoner. Considering I survived The Deep, it was damn near paradise.

"Listen, honey," Four-Eyes began and instantly became the one I wanted to hit more of the two. "We only need information. That's it. Just information. Like, what you are doing going after Cabot? What organization do you represent? Is this to set up a Califate or bring about the End Times? Or is it the fluffy bunnies you're trying to protect? Which one is it?"

I stared a hole into him so hard my eyes vibrated, and I thought for a moment I might be able to use the Force to make his heart explode out of his chest like in *Alien*.

Considering his weight-to-height ratio, his heart was heading that way anyway, and I would have given him a head start. Instead of taking the hint, he kept talking, adding more words I planned on stuffing back down his throat when I figured out how to get out of these zip-ties.

"You need to talk, darling." I shuddered again. There were going to be so many missing teeth… "You need to talk or else my friend here will make your jaw *incapable* of talking, do you understand?"

"Wait." I apparently surprised him by speaking. His late-night marathon cop shows probably never included a suspect smarter than them. "So, in order to get me to tell you why I followed Cabot here and broke into her room, you're going to *prevent me from talking*? Smart. Really smart."

This time, Four-Eyes got in on the action. A right cross whaled me on the eyebrow, and I felt blood trickle down the side of my face. Thankfully, it didn't run into my eye. I could deal with a trickle of blood on the side of my face, since it wouldn't be remotely the first time. These guys thought they were so tough. They had nothing on giant spider monsters.

"That's what you get for being sarcastic." He smugly sat back in his chair. I shook my head to clear what cobwebs hadn't been whacked out of me and looked up at him.

"So, I guess getting my lawyer is out of the equation," I sneered.

There was a moment of silence before Four-Eyes laughed. It was one quick laugh, but then after a second, another followed it. Then an entire series of them. Eventually, and confusedly, Haircut mimicked the laughter. It seemed like it was a completely foreign concept to him, and he was working out how the sound felt in his mouth before he let it out into the world.

He struck me as one of those 'energy is finite' kind of guys who detested doing anything other than what was absolutely necessary because he thought it would extend his life. Laughter must have been too big a waste for him.

"You're funny. Really funny. A lawyer." He turned to his buddy. "She wants her lawyer. Do you believe that?"

Before he could turn back to me, I figured I would get a piece of him in the one way I had available. They forgot to zip-tie my legs. Amateurs.

I threw my body weight and twisted in midair while aiming the heel of my foot for his groin. At the last second, I worried maybe he wasn't human and these were some kind of Far creatures after all, and his balls would be somewhere else entirely. Thankfully, when I made contact, those worries went away. A sound like an elephant having a heart attack came from his mouth as his cheeks filled with air and anguish. He fell over, and I struggled to my feet while spinning the chair so the legs were weapons and I whacked Haircut with them.

I spun back around and threw a kick low at him too, but he blocked it and swung. I ducked and tried to ram my head into his jaw. I almost missed, but got enough to knock him back a little. These guys were morons. If I had a few more minutes, I would knock them both out, get my hands free, get my hands on a weapon, then get out of here. Maybe after a few more kicks to Four-Eyes first, though.

I was getting the hang of chair-strapped-to-the-back

fighting when the door crashed open. My heart sank, and I stood there frozen for a second.

"No way," I muttered.

"Way," Bentham replied. Thrash smiled a megawatt smile and cracked his knuckles as he advanced on me. "Sara Slick, I'm taking you in."

CHAPTER NINETEEN

Before I could react, Thrash was on me, pushing me hard against the wall, and when I bounced back because of the legs, a fist the size of a Christmas ham came up in an uppercut to my jaw. I skidded back, trying to maintain my balance to no avail and went back, the chair hitting on its legs and sliding to a stop at the far wall. I saw stars in my vision and everything was cloudy when I heard Bentham's voice over the fog.

"Thrash, stop it! Cut it out. That's not what we're here for, and you know it," she chastised.

"Yeah, Thrash. Stop your infant punches and sit down like a good boy," I snapped before I could think better of it.

Blood sputtered from my lip as I spoke, and I was fairly sure most of that sounded like a mumble as my face swelled. I was sure I looked like I was someone allergic to seafood who won a shrimp-eating contest.

"One more word. I dare you. One more, and nobody stops me from ripping your head off," Thrash began, but Bentham was already between us and holding him back.

He had a mad glee in his eyes that told me his favorite kind of fight was at hand—one where the other person was mostly incapable of fighting back.

"Word," I murmured, and Thrash lived up to his name, thrashing around Bentham, trying to get around her. It took everything she had to keep us separated, and she eventually threw Thrash back against the wall and held out both hands between us.

"Everybody, shut up! Thrash, if you can't calm down, you need to go take a walk. Slick, I *am* curious to hear what you have to say, but if you make this any more difficult, I won't be anymore. Then Thrash and these two idiots can do whatever they want. Are we clear?" she asked.

I hated myself for it, but I nodded. She turned back to Thrash, who refused to make eye contact with her. His eyes were locked on me. Eventually, he nodded and Bentham seemed to relax a little.

"Fine. Good. All right, then. So, let's start over. Why were you after Cabot?" she questioned.

"I wasn't after her. I was trying to help her," I told her, conveniently leaving out the whole Far weapon I found under her pillow. The less Thrash and Bentham knew about my mission, the better.

"Trying to help her by stabbing her with a giant knife?" She pulled out the rune knife in a plastic bag from her briefcase.

I gaped at it but didn't say anything. If they wanted to pin me for this, I would take it. For now.

"Not mine." I tried to put my hands up in innocence. The zip-ties kind of ruined the effect.

There was silence for a moment as Bentham stared at

me, assuming I was going to continue my defense. When I didn't, she sighed and put the bag back down.

"Thrash, get these two out of here. I want to talk to her. You can come back when they're gone," she said.

Thrash looked at her like he was going to protest. Something about the way she looked back at him changed his mind, and he corralled the two men who were trying to get to their feet and figure out what had happened.

He escorted them to the door and went out with them and Bentham turned back to me. "Slick, you know the Philosophers Guild routinely monitors human law enforcement. As soon as your description came up, we were notified. You had to know this was a bad idea, but what I can't work out is, why did you do it?"

"Look." I stared directly into Bentham's eyes. Something about her made me think for once there might be someone who might listen beyond my small crew. Something about her knew that things weren't right, and if I could get through to her, it would make a difference. "I didn't come here to hurt anyone. I came here to help Cabot." At this point, Thrash walked back in and stood beside Bentham. Undeterred, I continued. "Bentham, listen to me. Cabot is in serious trouble. There are people out there who really do want to hurt her. I was only trying to help."

Before I finished the sentence, Thrash's fist crashed into my eyebrow. Bentham jumped up as he stepped back, blood on his fist, having opened my eye enough that I was sure it now looked like I was crying blood down my cheek. He held his hands up as Bentham walked him back.

"Liar," he yelled over her at me. "You're a liar and you

know it. You weren't here to help her, you were here to kill her. All for your sick game. You're a monster, Slick."

"If you hit her again, Thrash, I swear I will let her out of those zip ties and tell her to hit you back, do you understand?" Bentham threatened, inches from his face.

"What is wrong with you? This is Sara Slick. *The* Sara Slick. Why are you suddenly babying her?" he demanded.

Thrash's eyes narrowed as he looked at his partner, and there was a flicker of suspicion between them. I had to make some kind of play to get out of here before it got too serious, and Bentham was starting to look like my best hope. I figured it was worth a shot.

"Bentham, you have to believe me. If I wanted to kill Cabot, she would be dead. You know that. You have to help me get out of here and protect her, or else something terrible will happen to her," I appealed. "Hobbes is after her, which means she needs help."

"That's not my call," she told me, and I cocked my head to the side. On the one hand, it was an admission my case was being pled to someone who was listening. On the other, if she couldn't make that decision, that implied there was someone above her who could.

"Who can?" I asked.

"My boss. Our boss," she continued while looking at Thrash. As she said it, the door opened again, and a woman walked in.

She was tall and impressive, her hair in a neat bun above her and thin-rimmed glasses on her nose. She wore an expensive skirt and jacket combination and she walked into the room as confidently as any person had done anything in their life as far as I had ever seen. She exuded confidence and control.

"Bentham, Thrash." She acknowledged them with a nod, then pulled another chair across from me and sat, a folder stuffed with various papers in her hands.

She looked at me in silence for a moment, then slowly turned back to the other two. She cleared her throat, but nothing seemed to happen as they stared at her rather blankly.

"You can go now," she directed, with that executive smile people in power use when they're dismissing someone far below them. She turned back to me before they moved, and Bentham half-dragged Thrash out of the door. When the door shut, there was another moments' silence as we stared at each other. "Hello, Sara Slick, my name is Rand. I suppose you know about Philosophers?"

"Aristotle, Socrates, Plato, a couple of other morons I can't recall off the top of my head," I rattled off.

There was a curt smile, one without humor, and she seemed to reset and start again.

"I see your legendary sarcasm is still intact," she sneered.

"Legendary? I knew I was good," I began, but she cut me off.

"Enough." It was one word, but it carried so much weight. Unlike Bentham, when Rand said it, it really seemed like there was no argument to be made. It most certainly was enough.

"Yeah, I know about your Guild," I agreed. "A bunch of trumped-up fascists who claim to keep the peace but only succeed in keeping everyone afraid. Who do shit to protect anyone, except your asses."

"I know who you are as well, Sara Slickerman. You're a fraud," she said flatly.

I was genuinely offended for a moment. This was not how I expected this conversation to go. I got the impression a lot of people had that problem with Rand.

"A fraud?" I questioned.

"Yes. You purport to be so tough, so *special*, but we both know you wouldn't have lasted a single minute inside The Deep without the traitor Solon." Her expression grew darker.

My eyes opened wide, and I must have looked like a cartoon character. I was taken aback to hear Solon's name mentioned at all, much less as a traitor. What did she know about him?

"How do you know Solon?" I asked point-blank.

"Solon betrayed everything the Guild believes in. He allied himself with Nearsiders. He put our entire existence at risk and betrayed his kind. He was sick, and my only regret is I wasn't able to execute him myself. Unfortunately, the *Pax Philosophia* forbids that. At least that Nearside-loving traitor to his kind got lots of time to think about it while he rotted away in prison."

"You stop talking about him that way, or I will—" I began.

"You will what, exactly?" she inquired.

"Solon had some time in prison, that's true. Enough time to train me. Let me out of these zip-ties, and I'll show you how fucking well he did," I threatened.

Rand suddenly stood. For a moment, I thought I

convinced her to untie me, but instead she drew a deep breath and looked at me coldly. Her eyes were like icicles and her voice came out like the breath of a dragon. It burned so hot, you could almost see smoke.

"You know, I never believed you were guilty." My heart dropped. I couldn't believe I'd heard someone say that. A Philosopher, too. I wish I had recorded it, but what followed after made every joy of that moment shatter. "I never believed you were guilty at all, but I *did* send those Guild Agents to round up your father." Everything in my body went numb. "Maybe I will do so again. But right now, I have a duty to uphold. The *Pax Philosophia* will not be broken. Tell me now where your friends are, or face the consequences."

I sighed. I knew the game was up, that a life of rot awaited me in The Deep. But I'd gladly spend eternity in a cell than turn on my friends.

"Go to hell."

She smiled. "You first. You've been more than enough trouble since your escape to warrant it, regardless of your initial charges. Sara Slick, I hereby order your execution. Immediately. Bentham, Thrash! Come back in here," she called.

The door opened and the two agents came in hesitantly. Rand turned to them and handed Bentham a sheet of paper from her folder.

"What's this?" Bentham asked.

"Your official order. Signed by me." Her eyes cut back to me. "Take her out back and end her."

As Bentham held the note and Thrash started to laugh like a madman, Rand opened the door and slipped out, offering one last look back at me. She smiled, and I felt the evil radiate off her.

"Come along now," she said in a sing-song voice. "Time to end this stupid chapter in my life."

Then, she was gone.

CHAPTER TWENTY

Thrash looked nothing short of gleeful at the prospect of killing me. That wasn't good for my self-esteem. I mean, it wasn't that I hadn't encountered my share of people who found great joy in thoughts of grinding me up and turning me into filling for the Christmas pastries, but that was different. Thrash and I never spent days sharing a cell the size of an American Girl doll postage stamp, or been dropped down a chute into a gladiator ring together.

Bentham leaned close to Rand as her eyes flashed to me.

"With all due respect, an execution in this manner is against the law," she told her.

Oh, thank goodness.

"That law only applies to Farsiders," Rand snapped back. *Well, shit.* "Kill her now or lose your job."

That was a little depressing. Of all the times in the last ten years I had my life threatened or people had tried to kill me, it was never with the threat of unemployment dangling over them. According to Ally, it was a serious concern in these uncertain economic times. I didn't want to stand in the way of anyone's financial security or achieving the American dream or anything, but I definitely didn't want to be a footnote on a progress report, either.

Thrash didn't need any other encouragement. He pulled my switchblade from his pocket and severed the zip-ties securing me to the chair. The relief was momentary, since he quickly zipped my wrists together, then followed with my ankles.

He scooped me up and threw me backward over his shoulder so I hung upside down. I tried to lift myself up enough to see Bentham, but Thrash was too big to let me see over his shoulders. Instead, I twisted as I tried to reason with Bentham.

Thank the Universe for oblique muscles and the work-outs I randomly decided to do in the back of the RV.

Lift, twist, speak.

"Look, Bentham. Let's be reasonable."

Flat.

Lift, twist, speak.

"You don't have to do this."

Flat.

Lift, twist, speak.

"You know as well as I do this isn't the way things are supposed to be."

Flat.

At this point, Thrash jiggled me a few times to try to silence me. When everything in my head settled back to almost normal, I lifted and twisted again.

"You said it yourself in there. You aren't supposed to execute people like this."

Flat.

Lift, twist, speak. My muscles were getting tired, and there wasn't quite as much oomph in my twist anymore.

"Do you really want this to be the precedent you set? After all this time of being a loyal and effective Agent of the Guild, do you really want an illegal execution on your head?"

I could no longer do the lift and twist, so I resigned myself to dangling upside down and instead resorted to hand motions to underscore what I was saying. The zip-ties reduced their effectiveness, but it was better than spending my last moments doing an ab workout.

"We live in a time of personal responsibility, Bentham. You are what your actions speak. What do you want to say with the choices you make today?"

I threw my arms out to the sides for a dramatic finish. Well, I would have if they hadn't been zip-tied together.

"My duty is to the Guild," Bentham replied.

I wanted some sort of uprising. For the woman I saw in capris dancing at a music festival to find that glimmer of humanity inside herself and do what was right. The answer sucked all the life out of me, and I let my arms drop back so they dangled limply over my head. I let out a breath.

"Why were you really at that Festival?" I asked quietly.

Bentham had to take enough of a step ahead of Thrash that I could see her face and her cheeks flushed with embarrassment. She set her jaw and lifted her chin slightly.

"I really like Lizzo, and she was performing."

I already saw the flashes of truth inside Bentham. I knew she wasn't a bad person, not really. Underneath the robes and all the pomp and circumstance, there was a real person in there, and this only humanized her more.

"Come on, Bentham. This doesn't have to go down like this," I implored. "Tell the goon to put me down, I'll run away, and you can tell Rand I overcame you with some unimaginable force and escaped. You don't even have to tell him to put me down. Kick him in the back of the knee and I'll wriggle free."

"I'm sorry, Sara," she whispered.

Thrash walked me outside into the night air. Above me, the sky glittered with a thick sprinkling of stars, and the full moon looked impossibly big. Its light was so bright it washed out the stars immediately around it, so the sky looked empty and endlessly deep. Up until then, I'd been trying to hold myself up at least some to stop the bouncing and flailing as Thrash walked. Now I let myself go dead-weight and sagged from his shoulder. If he was going to haul me to my death, he would have to work for it.

We made our way to a secluded spot, and Thrash unceremoniously let go of me. For a second, I hovered over his shoulder, somehow perfectly balanced so I didn't go either way. He poked me in the foot and shoved me backward so I toppled to the ground. My shoulder ached where I made impact, but I figured there was a lot more I needed to worry about soon, so there was no point in stressing too much about some bumps and bruises.

I quickly got to my feet. They might be preparing to execute me, but they weren't going to do it while I was curled up on the ground in front of them. I wasn't going out like a punk. Bentham reached into her robes and pulled out a large, shiny axe. The curved executioner's blade glinted in the moonlight and seemed to connect seamlessly with the handle.

"Holy hell. Where did you get that thing? Have you been walking around with it in your pocket this entire time? That is a seriously utilitarian robe design." It wasn't the best time to talk, but I couldn't help myself.

Bentham adjusted her grip on the axe, but hesitated. Thrash reached out and grabbed it from her, then raised it gleefully over his head. The sparkle in his eyes said he was ready to enjoy this. His muscles flexed as his grip tightened and he drew a deep breath as he gathered strength. I closed my eyes and waited for the rush of cool air that I figured would run down my back and shoulders when my head was no longer connected to them.

Ally's face popped up in my mind, my subconscious tossing up one last image of something wonderful before I died. Then my father's replaced it. It was from a rainy day when I was nine and he grabbed me and took me outside to dance in the puddles. The rain cascaded off his thick mustache and flattened his hair to his skull.

Thrash let out a roar as he pulled the axe down, and time slowed. These were my last moments, and I watched, fascinated as he moved as if in slow motion, his arms extending as the axe moved from behind him to above him, and eventually would move to in front of him and down into me. Suddenly, an arrow sliced through the air in front of me and hit Bentham. The impact knocked her down, and she grunted.

Thrash turned to look at her, and in the moment of

confusion, the world returned to full speed. He stumbled as the momentum took him off-course and the axe buried into the ground beside me. Another arrow zipped through the air, and it sizzled as it struck the brick wall behind Thrash.

They were electrified and looked rather nasty, and Bentham twitched on the ground as the arrow in her shoulder produced a growing pool of blood and occasional sparks. I shouldered forward, smashed into Thrash, and snatched the axe from his hand. Archie and Pip ran out from somewhere to one side. I looked at the impressive crossbow in his hands and nodded.

"Nice. I haven't seen that one before," I complimented.

"It's new," he acknowledged. "Seemed to work pretty well."

Thrash came at me again, and Pip lunged for the much larger creature. She leapt into the air while aiming her body into his center mass. He swatted at her like a fly. His hand made contact, and she soared back in the other direction. I was worried about her, but as soon as she hit the ground, she bounded right back up.

I got the feeling she wasn't a stranger to being tossed around. She said she was the smallest of her kind, which probably translated into being used as a toy more often than she would have liked. If there was a threshold for how often you can be used as a ball in a game of catch and thought it was acceptable.

The monstrous Guild Agent had turned to watch her fly through the air and bounce on the ground, so he wasn't paying close enough attention to me. When he stepped toward Pip, I swung the butt of the axe around and caught him on the side of the head.

Thrash stumbled a little and I lifted the axe as high as I could, then brought the blunt end down hard on the juncture right between his shoulder and neck. This made his knees buckle. As soon as he crashed down, I whacked him under the chin with the flat side of the blade. He smashed down to the ground.

"You don't mind if I take this?" I hissed as I pulled my switchblade out of his pocket right before we all ran.

I didn't leave the axe. That thing was mine now. I followed close behind Archie as we ran through the streets and eventually toward a van seeming to wait for us at a corner.

"Thanks for saving my skin back there," I told them. "And everything contained within. How did you find me?"

As I said it, the door on the side of the van slid open and Dog looked out at me. This wasn't Dog the shaggy black creature I had drugged and gripped for dear life on the airplane. This was Dog in human form, as sleek and handsome as ever. Seeing him took me a little aback, and our eyes lingered on each other for a brief moment before he reached out and wrapped his hand around my wrist.

With a yank, he pulled me into the van with him. Pip and Archie piled in after me and slammed the sliding door shut. We arranged ourselves on the seats and hooked our seatbelts, although that seemed a tad ridiculous considering the circumstances.

"I'm sorry I wasn't out there," Dog apologized. "My injuries from the last fight still haven't healed as well as I'd like. If they were, I would have jumped in there with you."

"I know," I told him.

"Are we ready?"

I looked up and saw Ally peering at me in the rearview mirror from where she sat behind the wheel. I nodded, and we took off down the street.

"You really are building up quite the collection of near-death experiences," Ally commented. "They seriously did a number on you."

I hissed as she dabbed more rubbing alcohol on the deep gash of my split eyebrow. I knew I wasn't exactly at my best right now. A single glimpse of myself in the mirror was enough to confirm everything I felt. I had been beaten up pretty bad, some of it probably happening while I was still unconscious. Unconscious or not, I felt every punch and bounce against Thrash's back. Still, it wasn't at the top of the list in terms of awful things I'd been through.

"I've had worse," I told her.

"How much worse?" Pip asked.

I looked at her out of the corner of my eye. "This is permanent press tumble dry at home compared to the heavy-duty towel load at an industrial laundry."

"Wow," the lizard girl said.

"I'll stick with dry cleaning," Ally said through a grimace

as she tossed a bloodied cotton ball in the trash can at her feet and reached for a butterfly bandage.

"How are you doing over there, Archie?" I asked.

Since we got back to the flat, he'd been hard at work on his runes. He seemed driven, with more enthusiasm than I had seen in him in a long time. He lifted his head and nodded.

"I'm working on something that could be amazing. I have this new idea based on how well Cabot was able to take you down," he told me.

"Glad to be your inspiration." I adjusted into more of a sitting position on the couch so I could watch what he was doing more closely. "You know, you should maybe consider sticking to some of the more traditional weapons sometimes. You looked like a serious badass with that crossbow."

Ally grinned. "That was my idea."

"It was?" I asked.

"Absolutely. You gotta have a crossbow if vampires are loose." She waved her hand around like she was gesturing at a bunch of little vampires jumping around in front of her before she put the butterfly bandage in place over my eyebrow and smoothed it onto my skin.

"Well, I can't argue with that. But I still want to know how the hell you found me. I didn't know where they brought me. How did you know?" I asked.

From where he sat on a chair diagonal to the couch, Dog turned his dark eyes to me.

"I have your scent," he murmured in a low voice.

I waited for him to say something more, but he left it at that. My heart jumped a little, and I turned to the rest of them to try to ignore it.

"Thank you. All of you, really. I would absolutely be a goner if you guys weren't there to save me. And the part that would piss me off the most is Thrash would have been the one to smear me across the ground. But I got to keep his axe, so sucks for him." I grinned and winced at a sharp pain through my eyebrow. It was worth it.

"I'm glad we found you in time," Archie said.

Splinter scrambled up my leg and onto my chest. I nuzzled him. He pulled his hand from behind his back and stuffed a crunchy snack food of some kind into my mouth.

"I'm glad you got cheese-drunk and stayed in the flat before I wrapped that firehose around my waist," I told him. "There's no telling what might have happened to you if they found you. Besides, we were really high up, and you get sick with heights. You'd have left me for Ally, wouldn't you, you adorable little traitor?"

I nuzzled his head. It was pretty obvious what would have happened to him, but I didn't want to think about it. He tucked his head under my chin and let out a little sigh that rumbled in his chest, almost like a purr. I rested my head against his and closed my eyes.

"What's wrong?" Ally asked. "I mean, other than you got the living snot beaten out of you and a big axe swung at your head. Is there something else?"

"I'm a little upset," I admitted.

"Why?" she asked.

"We're no closer to helping Senator Cabot. She'll never trust us now. Not after that fiasco." I let out a long breath.

"Well..." Ally glanced over at Archie, who returned her

look. Something passed between them without either saying anything.

"What was that?" I asked. "Well, what?"

Ally looked back at me and let out a breath. This was one of those moments when a little voice in the back of my head started saying 'she's your best friend, she wouldn't betray you. She's your best friend, she wouldn't betray you. She's your best friend, she wouldn't betray you.'

"It turns out Cabot was never going to trust you," she continued.

"What?" My eyes widened.

"Because that's not Cabot," Dog told me.

"Explain," I asked sharply, my head snapping to the side to look at him.

Ally opened her computer on the coffee table and started searching through it.

"I tried to warn you earlier, but I failed. It's why I sought you out. That vampire was nothing compared to the real threat here. Shapeshifters."

Stunned by the revelation, I sat and processed for a few seconds before I could speak again.

"How did you know?" I finally asked.

"My people have their ways."

"You have your ways about a lot of things, don't you?"

"We do. And we also hate Shapeshifters. They aren't like us. They don't change form because it's part of them. They don't go from a human-like form to an innate animal form. These are ugly, disgusting creatures that shift into looking like whoever they desire. They steal the faces of whomever they wish so they can use their appearance to manipulate others and get what they want. It's cruel and it's dangerous. They're able to look like anyone, which means they can infiltrate themselves into anyone's life, take anyone's place, and do anything while blaming it on someone else."

"They could get away with anything," I muttered.

"It isn't only that. Yes, they can take someone else's face and use it so no one knows they're committing crimes or anything else they might want to do. But they could also choose a person's face specifically so they can blame that person for what they did. If they want people to believe someone did something, they can make that happen very easily," Dog said.

"Like with Cabot," I concluded.

"Exactly," he confirmed.

I shook my head. "I don't understand."

Ally spun her computer around so I could see the screen. It was a paused video that looked like it was taken during the peace summit.

"Watch carefully," Ally instructed.

She started the video and a voice crackled through from somewhere off-screen.

"Senator Bryce Cabot."

The tall, stately woman strode across the stage toward another ambassador—some Russian dude, flanked on the right by an attractive, well-dressed man who could have been his twin and was probably his assistant. The woman smiled as she extended her hand.

"That's Cabot." I pointed at the screen.

"Yeah, that's what the announcer said," Ally muttered. "Keep watching."

My best friend allowed the video to continue for a few

more seconds until the two world leaders clasped hands, and something stood out to me.

"What was that?" I asked.

Ally looked at Dog, then back at me. "Did you see something?"

"Maybe. I don't know. Can you go back a few seconds and play it again?" She played the video again, and again something struck me, but I couldn't place exactly what it was. She went through it twice more before I spoke. "Hold on. Go back about ten seconds and stop right when they shake hands and the camera focuses on Cabot."

Ally played it back to the right point, then froze the video. I stared at the screen, trying to see what my mind was trying to figure out from the footage. Cabot's hair looked kind of flat from this angle. Her suit might have fit better a few pounds ago, but that could be fixed by taking it in. Her face looked a little strange. I kept examining it and I went back to her face looking strange. There was no other way to describe it. She simply looked...off. Like she had a glitch. Then it hit me. Her eyes. They flashed red. It only lasted for a second, but in the freeze frame, the color was more obvious.

"Holy shit," I muttered.

"Yeah," Ally said.

"But why? Why would a Shapeshifter want to impersonate Cabot?" I asked.

"What better way to destroy world peace?" Pip asked.

"The war," I realized. "The war Pip heard them talking about. They don't want to start a war for themselves. They don't want something small. They want to create a massive, large-scale war and let the world burn itself to the ground." Then it dawned on me. "Cabot."

"What about her?" Ally asked. "You saw her. At least what's supposed to be her. A creature wearing her face."

"Right. We've been operating this whole time under the belief that Hobbes and his minions were targeting Cabot for an attack." I shook my head. "That's not what's going on. They weren't planning on attacking Cabot, because they already stole her face."

"What do you think they're doing? Why did the Shapeshifter choose to look like her?" Archie asked.

"Like Dog said. Shifting to look like someone else isn't always about not wanting the blame not put on them, but the blame being put specifically on someone else. They took her face so they could blame her for something. I think they're going to have Cabot kill the Russian ambassador."

I looked back at the screen and the Russian smiling at who he thought was Cabot. There was nothing but trust in that expression. He had no idea he was looking right into the face of an imposter.

"We thought Hobbes was going to murder Cabot and reveal The Far to the world. But he wants the human world to tear itself apart."

"But why?" Pip asked.

"What better way to prepare a society for an invasion?" Ally grumbled under her breath.

"Divide and conquer," Archie finished for her.

Dog suddenly cocked his head.

"What? What is it?" I asked.

"We're not alone," Dog grumbled somewhere in his throat.

Pip ran over to the window and peered out. She reached back and gestured for me to join her. As soon as I got within a few feet of the window, I knew what she was staring at. I saw the flashing lights.

"Shit. It's the cops," I grumbled. "We're surrounded."

"What do we do?" Ally asked, panicked.

"We have to get out of here," Archie said. "And if there are any of them left alive, we need to make sure they don't follow us."

"Absolutely not," I refused, the words flying out of me with far more emotion than I intended. "We won't kill any of them. Not a single one. They think they're doing their job. Protect and serve and all that. I'll have to fight my way out, yes, and it won't be pretty, but I won't kill any of those humans and neither should any of you."

"Then what's the plan?" Pip asked. I turned to her and tried to think. This would be hard, but I had to try.

"I'll distract them. It'll be a fight and it will get ugly, but I think I can keep from hurting anyone too badly with this thing." I tested the weight of the axe in my hands. "I'll draw them away from the building, and you guys scatter. Go in as many directions as possible, and make it look like you're running away from the fight like you have nothing to do with it. We can meet somewhere in a few hours when I can shake them."

"How? You don't know where you are or where you're running to. How will you ditch twenty cops who are looking for you?" Ally asked.

"This might help." Archie held up a glove. I stared at it for a moment, then at Archie.

"Didn't you say that it wasn't ready?" I asked. "Also, what the hell is it?"

"Well, no, not technically. It has a design that allows it to send electric shocks along with added force to punches and grip. I call it 'The Light Touch.'" He looked at the glove like he wasn't sure what it would do at any moment. "It might not be ready. Or it might be. Or it might work way better than it's supposed to, which is not working the right way in any case. Frankly, Slick, I have no idea what it will do, but it couldn't hurt to have it on."

"Archie, if I use that thing, will it set off a nuclear explosion or kill all the electricity in the city?" I asked.

"Probably not," he admitted.

I sighed. "Fine, give it to me."

I placed the glove on my hand and marveled at its weight. It felt tight and flexible, but there was a little added "oomph" to it. Even if the taser part didn't work, it would be helpful to have a little extra power in my punches.

I looked around at my friends and tried to take the moment in. A little while ago, I was being beaten up and about to be split in two by Thrash. Now I had his axe, and my friends saved me. Comparatively, running from the cops should be a breeze, but if I were to be honest, I was pretty tired already.

"We should meet up somewhere easy to find. What about Picadilly Circus?" Dog suggested.

I nodded. "Good as anywhere here, I guess. You guys scatter. We'll meet there."

A sound crashed from a door somewhere below. The cops were breaking into the building.

"Go, get out of here. Make it look like you're running from trouble," I demanded, and the group took off. I opened the window to the fire stairs and made a decision. If they were going to get me, it was going to be in style. I drew a breath and climbed out.

After I went down one floor, I noticed that the window two floors below me was open. The only problem was there was already a policeman heading past it toward me. As he rounded the corner, I connected with him by smashing the handle of the axe into his stomach, then grabbed him by the back of the shirt and his belt to ram him into the wall of the building with my free hand. He slumped and I rushed past him, hoping he would stay down long enough for me to get down and into that room before he called for backup.

I made it to the window without incident and slipped in, finding myself in a bedroom. The room was empty, and I rushed through it to the door leading out into the hallway. When I got there, two more cops were heading toward me.

They seemed surprised I was coming toward them, as if they thought they were sweeping an empty room. I ducked under the outstretched arm and threw myself at the cop behind him in the narrow hallway. I elbowed him in the jaw, then spun and smashed the other in the face with my fist.

A couple of rapid-fire kicks to the stomach knocked him back. I spun back to knee his partner in the stomach, and when he bent over, did a knee lift to his jaw. He flew back and slammed into the wall, and I laid in a few punches until he slid all the way down. The first one recovered enough to try calling on his shoulder radio.

I snatched the cord and yanked, separating it from the radio, then spun into a kick to his head. He launched back toward the door of the bedroom unconscious and I put my hands on my knees to breathe.

I only had a second to rest since more sounds came from everywhere. Somewhere in the distance, Archie's unmistakable voice yelled out in the worst English accent I ever heard that he was trying to get out of their way. It made me smile, but I hoped it would work. He sounded like Arnold Schwarzenegger doing a Michael Caine impression.

I ran for the door and saw a cop holding Archie by the shirt. He was obviously suspicious of him, but seeing me changed his priorities. As he let go of Archie's shirt, I flung the blunt end of the axe at his face and he fell backward. He tumbled toward the railing of the long stairwell and crashed through it. I grabbed him as he was about to fall to his doom and yanked him toward me while ducking and rolling to the side. He crashed into the room I came from and I followed him in, curb stomping him into the floor.

Not bothering to wait around and see if he got up, I tore back out of the room and into the stairwell. There were cops above and below me, but it looked like Archie and the rest of the group had made it. Now I needed to escape and get to the streets. I ran down a flight of stairs, reached another door and tried the handle. It was locked, so I kept moving. Another floor and another door that was locked shut. One of these doors would either be unlocked or have to be kicked in. My best bet was to make it to the fire stairs again and get to the alley behind the building.

One more floor, and this time a cop reached it the same time I did. He swung first, trying to hit me with a baton that I dodged. I ducked below and swung a punch to his chest. It was now or never for the taser glove, and I flicked my wrist like Archie showed me to activate it. A loud whirring sound emanated from it and the cop's eyes bulged as I smiled. I thrust forward and pressed it to his chest.

Nothing.

Worse than nothing—the whirring sputtered and stopped. The cop and I both looked down at it in confusion, then at each other, and back at it. I shrugged and flung the crown of my head at him, hitting him under the jaw and knocking him out cold where he stood. Before he could hit the floor, I kicked him down the stairs where he barreled into a couple other cops and knocked them down like the world's weirdest bowling game ever.

I spun and kicked the door, and it flew open easily. I ran across to the first window I saw, then jumped and crashed through it, not bothering to think until too late that I didn't know if the ladder was waiting outside it. I fell down an entire flight before I swung my axe out and caught the railing. My body jerked hard as I held on for dear life several floors above the concrete.

I let go with one hand and climbed up and onto the

railing, then over to get on the stairs. It didn't seem like any other cops were coming this way, and I ran down the stairs as fast as I could. When I was on the second level, I took my shot and leapt from the railing and onto the concrete below. As I landed on my feet, I heard the sirens behind me and knew they were coming. I needed to get going.

I took off down the first alley and darted to the left when it split. It split again and I went right, and quickly realized my mistake. Feet pounded behind me and whistles blew to alert me to stop. And I was in a dead end, stopped by a tall chain-link fence and buildings on both sides. I spun and waited.

There were likely two choices—using the axe or punching my way out. When the cops arrived, there were three of them, and punching my way out looked less likely. These were three, large, unhappy cops, and I was damn tired. I reached for the axe again when a whirring sound started. I looked at my hand and saw the glove glowing.

What the hell, it was worth a shot. I reached out and grabbed the first cop. A bolt of electricity shot out of my hand and the cop shook hard, then fell over. The other two stared in shock, and one reached for his hip. I knew what that meant, and I flung myself at him, smashing my elbow into his face before laying my buzzing hand on his chest. The third cop was yelling into his shoulder mic when I reached out and grabbed his leg, shocking him and knocking him out cold.

With three cops sprawled at my feet, I stood gingerly and tried to figure out what was next. I heard traffic coming from behind me and I decided to get out any way possible. I scaled the chain link fence, went over and landed on the ground outside it, free from police and on my way to escape.

CHAPTER TWENTY-THREE

After sneaking around a building, I found myself on a side street on the other end of the neighborhood. I ducked under the line of concrete that separated me from being seen by those on the street and tried to half-run, half crab-walk my way to another alley. I was safer in them since even if there were bad guys hanging around, all I had to do was fight.

Out in the open, anyone who glimpsed my bruised, swollen, and bloody mug would have a good idea that I was up to some trouble and liable to call the cops. I also carried a rather concerning-looking axe, which I was sure would draw some attention as well. I debated ditching it in a trash can, but two things stopped me. One, I really, really liked it and two, if I ran into trouble again, I'd kick myself for losing it. When stuck between a rock and a hard place, I figured I'd go with whichever one kept an axe in my hand.

I realized rather suddenly, as I tucked and rolled past a break in the concrete, that I had no idea exactly where Piccadilly Circus was. Or what it was, for that matter. I had a vague understanding that it was not, in fact, a literal circus where dill pickles were on display in new, strange, and horrifying manners. Other than that, it was all context clues, and the only context I had right now was that it was a physical place, and everyone seemed to know about it.

Ahead of me at an intersection, was a police car with several cops crowded around it, seemingly uninterested in doing anything in particular except running out the clock while other cops did the heavy lifting. Lifting that likely included finding me. I couldn't simply walk past them, so I figured I would cross the street going the other way and make my way down an alley on that side instead.

I stepped into the road and was very rudely reminded that checking traffic was a little different than back home as a car blared toward me, the driver laying on his horn, from the opposite direction of where I thought it would be.

I snapped my eyes back to the cops and saw one of them vaguely look in my direction, but then go back to his conversation. I released a breath I didn't know I was holding and looked for traffic correctly this time. When I saw an opening, I tried to walk across as casually as possible. When I finally reached the other side and got into the alley, I bolted, running like my ass was on fire. After a few blocks, a dozen or so turns down new alleys, and at least one puddle of what looked like ancient, stagnant rain, I was positive that I'd shaken any trace of a dragnet set out for me.

I was also positive that I was completely, totally, helplessly lost.

The area I had wandered was more industrial and less populated, which usually meant trouble. It was exactly the kind of place I would expect Archie to have a friend of a friend of a coworker of a friend who sold Farside stuff. Since I didn't have much choice, I tried to follow the buildings back out to a street where I could find someone or something to tell me where I was and how to get where I was going. But one miscalculated turn, and I was now in the dankest, darkest, most decrepit of alleys, and a sound behind me let me know I wasn't alone.

At this point, I had fought so many people today that I was simultaneously in need of a sit-down and about ready to straight-up murder the first person who cut the wrong expression at me. I was tired, hungry, kind of sleepy, bruised to hell, and I knew for absolute certain that I smelled bad. If I didn't get into a shower, put on some comfy sweatpants, and eat a taco in the next few hours, I was likely to use the first tool Archie made that might have a nuclear reaction in hopes it had one.

The sound behind me intensified as more things were knocked around. My ears were tuned in to hear footsteps, but whoever was behind me was being careful not to make any. Either they were Far creatures or literal ninjas, because the only noises being made were small and seemingly accidental. After years in The Deep, I got used to small sounds equaling big problems, but whoever it was likely thought they were following me without being noticed.

I kept them coming, walking fast enough to set a decent pace, but slow enough they could tail me. If I could make it deep enough into the alley, I could dispatch them, maybe force some information about where the hell I was out of them, and get out of there.

Finally, when I felt I had gotten them deep enough into the alley to not arouse suspicion from the street, I spun. Something smartass was on the tip of my tongue, but as soon as I scanned what followed me, it went away into a whiff of lost one-liners and unrepressed sarcasm. I searched my brain for a word to convey the sense of surprise, dread, and frustration at how stupid I had been and only came up with one.

"Fuck."

Standing before me were three vampires, weak ones, but ones who could cause some damage. I knew where these guys came from and why they were after me. This meeting was no accident. The big slashing "SS" in the chest of each one of them had the marks of a dueling sword. Like the one the assassin used. Each of them looked like they had been turned fairly recently and were still getting the hang of their new life. Or unlife, as it were. Dead life? The vocabulary here was confusing.

Nevertheless, word was somehow spreading fast that I was in town.

One of them shuffled a step closer to me, and I realized he wasn't actually touching the ground. That would account for the lack of footsteps. They all three floated inches above the concrete—enough to hit a can or a bottle lying on the ground, but not enough for their shoes to make scraping sounds while they followed. Oddly, this made me feel a little better. At least I wasn't losing my ability to hear people walking behind me.

Right when I'd started to figure out a plan for the three vampires, a sound behind me startled me enough to spin to it and my heart sank. There were four others behind me. I was surrounded by low-level vampires, all most likely under the control of an assassin who I had royally pissed off, and now not only had a contract on my ass but a grudge too. An axe to grind.

Axe.

Holy shit, I still had the axe. I yanked it from my back, where I had slung it using its leather strap, and armed myself with it in a manner that was simultaneously backing up and challenging them to charge me. I tried to back up toward the concrete, not the building closest, so I could make a mad dash for any door I saw if things got too hairy.

I spun the axe in my hand, finally ready to use the blade for its intended purpose as they closed in around me. One made the first move and paid for it. The axe split him down the middle, and while I used a lot of energy for that shot, it was worth it to see the sudden realization and fear in the eyes of the other ones. It wasn't clear to me how much coherent thought a newly made vampire was capable of, but I saw by their reaction to their dead colleague that they were aware of fear. I pulled the axe back to me as I let the split torso of the first vampire fall on the ground and looked at them.

"Who's next?" I invited.

Three of them charged at once, and I swung low, arching up. I connected with all three in various areas, the first in the knees, separating one leg and slicing a great chunk out of the other. The next got caught at his hip and crossed over his chest to his shoulder, and both of them hit the ground in shock and disbelief. The third one wasn't so lucky.

As his body tumbled toward me, his head fell off and rolled behind him. The body crashed into the wall and slumped, squirting blood high into the air and making a red rain shower down on the rest of us. The head rolled to a stop next to the one whose torso was badly cut and a dull, monotone scream came out of it.

There were three left, but I felt a lot better about them now. All three charged at once, fanning out so I couldn't hit them in one blow. One reached for my arm and got hit by the sudden whirring of my shock glove, which sent him flying backward while sparks flew out of him. Another tried to grab my axe and wrestle it away from me while the third tried to get me from behind.

I temporarily let go of the axe with one hand to elbow the one behind me, then reached to grab it again. The vampire pulled it up, and I suddenly hung a foot off the ground. It opened its wide mouth, and fangs gnawed after me. I dropped my grip on the axe and fell to the ground, opting to punch it as hard as I could with the shock glove.

The vampire shook violently, and the axe fell from its hand. I caught it on the way down and swung without looking behind me. The blade caught the vampire charging me from behind in the neck and stuck there. I slowly turned my head to see him, my hand on the chest of one, electrocuting him until he smelled like frying meat, and the other holding an axe buried deep in his throat.

Finally, I let go of the hold with the glove and grabbed the axe with both hands. I yanked it out of his neck and watched them both crumple to the ground. I drew a deep breath as I looked at them all around me in various states of deader than undead and still sort of breathing undead.

I needed to finish them. I walked up to the first one, who I had buried the axe into his neck, and slammed the blade down to decapitate him. I repeated this for all the others, and when I was done, I was absolutely soaked in blood, tired, and angry. The only bright side was that after all that, I suddenly wasn't all that hungry anymore.

CHAPTER TWENTY-FOUR

When I was five years old, my father brought me to the circus. It sounds like the beginning of a dramatic and deeply introspective college entrance essay question. This would be the point when I should start waxing poetic about feeling like the tiger leaping through the rings of fire, fearing men in red coats because of the patriarchal oppression of the ringmaster, and getting my first makeup tips from the clowns. But, bear with me, that's not where we're headed.

Although, there might have been a few months in high school when I was first allowed to wear makeup and thought blue was a valid shade for all eye makeup requirements from shadow to liner to mascara.

Anyway, when I was five years old, my father brought me to the circus. It was the most incredible thing I'd ever seen. A contortionist in a bright pink bodysuit turned herself into a wheel and rolled around one of the rings, then rode standing up on the back of an elephant. A group of men built themselves up into a tower and deposited another woman on a high wire. I ate approximately my weight in cotton candy and peanuts. It was nothing short of magical.

Of course, now that I was out of The Deep, I might want to question circuses and the issues with animal rights. Not to mention the sheer terror factor of that many clowns bubbling out of the back of a tiny car like an Alka-Seltzer of the damned. That put a touch of a damper on the joy and whimsy of my memories of that trip with my dad, and I never ended up going back. But I still remembered how much I loved that first afternoon under the Big Top.

So, when we decided to meet up at Piccadilly Circus, I was stoked. I was confident by now the problematic elements of the show were gone, and I had a serious hankering for a big fluff of pink cotton candy. Had to be pink. Blue cotton candy was only for heathens and the Ferris wheel at the middle school fall festival. That day was a pink cotton candy type of day.

It goes without saying I was a little bummed when I got directions from a shopkeeper closing up late who was willing to overlook the blood and ended up running into what was decidedly not a circus. There was no huge tent, no smell of popcorn, and no gasps of fear from the audience that the people swinging on the trapeze would miss their catch, but secretly kind of hoping they'd get to see them fall.

Instead, I walked out into a large open space in the middle of a circle of buildings. A few people meandered around in the shadows of the dark lessened by the lights around the edge.

Without a phone or any other way to contact them, I

had no choice but to wander around until I caught sight of Ally, Archie, and Pip. I did that, part searching out my group and part taking in my surroundings. This might be my only chance to visit London, and it might not be the most leisurely of experiences, but I was going to make the most of it.

The late hour meant there weren't a ton of people, but the crowd was still enough that I had to weave through people as I made my way across the stones. There seemed to be a combination of commuters who worked late, locals headed somewhere, and tourists. Yet, somehow, it didn't have the same feeling of the tourist spots throughout the city and in other places. There wasn't anything overtly shiny and manipulative about the place, which was saying a lot considering the massive billboards and neon lights flashing the names of local businesses.

Instead, it almost felt overlooked, like the people moving around in it didn't see it. It was the same kind of effect as people who lived near national monuments or natural wonders. Eventually, you see it so many times it doesn't really matter anymore. That was nice in a way. It meant those amazing things got to be so much of a part of their lives they were used to it.

At the same time, it was sad. Nothing as beautiful or as astonishing, if confusing, as places like this should be overlooked. Not me. I knew what it was like to have the ability to see things like this taken away from me. Everything taken away from me. Now that I was out, I was going to absorb everything like a sponge, appreciate it all, and never lose sight of how incredible the world around me was.

Starting immediately. Wow. That was a gorgeous fountain. It had absolutely no place in a circus, but it was stunning. Even the statue of the winged archer on top made me a little nostalgic, remembering Ally's encounter with the Angel, and Archie coming into my almost execution with crossbow blazing. Even Pip stared up at it like it was speaking to her in some way.

Pip. I found Pip!

Not that she blended all that well. They had her in a new human disguise, and if anything, it was worse than the first. The rune Archie made came from a good place in his heart, but rather than really making her look like a human, it made her look vaguely humanoid. Of course, I might only have been able to see it because I knew it was there.

It was entirely possible a woman no more than three feet tall would throw on a dress, bad makeup, and a floppy hat and rock it out with her swagger down the street. But that swagger came from her still not being able to walk with her tail strapped to her leg. And if the floppy hat fell off, I wasn't convinced anyone who passed by wouldn't be able to see her spiky little lizard head sticking up from her awkward-fitting dress.

"Were you trying to confuse me by telling me to go to a circus that isn't a circus?" I stepped up beside Pip.

She turned and gasped when she saw me.

"Slick!" she exclaimed.

"Shh," I quieted her by holding my finger to my lips and looking around to make sure no one was descending on us.

"Sorry, Slick!" she whispered.

"Perfect." I flashed her a thumbs-up.

Ally and Archie ran around either side of the fountain

toward me, and Ally gathered me into her arms for a tight hug. Dog followed closely behind and seemed to grin as Ally tightened her chokehold around my neck and began to sway.

"I'm so glad you're ok," she gushed, then finally let go and gave me a chance to breathe without complications.

"What is this place? I thought we were going to see a tightrope or eat some peanuts or something. It's not a circus," I complained.

"It is a circus," Ally corrected.

I looked around. "Do you see a ringmaster anywhere? This place looks like Times Square and Central Park had a baby."

"I don't see a ringmaster, but I do see a circus," Ally insisted.

"Where?" I asked.

"You're standing in it. The circle around the fountain." She gestured around at it.

I glared at her. "That is a mean trick."

She slung her arm around my shoulders. "Don't worry, I'm sure we can find you some peanuts somewhere."

"I think right now we have more to worry about than peanuts," Archie reminded us. "We're dealing with some serious problems and we need to figure out what we're going to do about them."

We sat on the steps leading up to the fountain, and Ally glanced back at it.

"Did you know people used to drink out of this?" she asked. "There were cups, and people could come get a drink of water while walking through the city."

"Oh." I looked over my shoulder at the water tumbling

through the basins. "That's fascinating. What happened to the cups?"

"They got stolen. And the original design for the fountain was different, and the guy who designed it got so mad they changed it, he wouldn't even come to the dedication." She nodded solemnly.

I gave her a "Wow," for effect.

"Do you think we could focus?" Archie demanded. "I don't know about the two of you, but I'd like to get this done and not have a world war on our hands at the end of it."

"Sorry," Ally and I told him simultaneously.

I leaned to the side toward her without taking my eyes off Archie.

"What happened?" I asked out of the corner of my mouth.

"There was a flaw in how they changed the design and it soaked everybody," she replied.

"Whoa."

"So, what we figured out so far is an influential world leader has been replaced by a Shapeshifter who stole her face and is now gearing up for war. Speaking of which, Slick, can you do something about the blood?" Archie nodded at me.

I looked down at my clothes. The benefit of not having the people moving around the area seeming too invested in what was going on around them was that I didn't inspire any screams or stampedes.

"What is it you want me to do? I don't think London is ready to be converted into a nudist colony."

"All right. We have to get fresh clothes. But we need to

be careful. The cops are following the command of the Shapeshifter, which means we aren't safe anywhere. They'll do anything they think the Senator tells them to. Which means they won't believe a word we say and will keep coming after us. A compulsion they currently share with the Philosophers," Archie pointed out.

"They know we're here, and they'll come after us. I'm sure they aren't particularly happy about my little run-in with Bentham and Thrash. Rand was fairly insistent about taking me out and threatened Bentham's position with the Guild if she didn't come back with my head on a stake. Actually, she didn't say anything about my heart being on a stake. But the threat was there. I saw it in her eyes."

"Your head on a stake...now that would be something to see," Pip pointed out with altogether too much excitement for the topic of conversation.

"Thank you, Pip. I appreciate the note." I gave a tight smile.

She leaned over and splashed her hand in the water of the fountain, contented with her contribution to the conversation. At the sound of the splashing, Splinter wriggled out into the open and performed a formless dive that quickly turned into a belly-flop into the water. Another reason it was good there weren't many people still wandering the streets this late at night. I didn't want anyone to see him and think the bubonic plague was about to rise again.

"If we don't figure this out, the humans could descend into all-out war." I watched Splinter swim around happily to take some sting out of the words.

"And that would further set up humanity to fail when the Farsiders attack," Archie pointed out.

"So, what do we do?" Ally asked.

I looked up at her. "We do what we have to. We kick their asses."

CHAPTER TWENTY-FIVE

I pressed my back against the wall and scooted a few steps to the side, then paused, looked to either side and scooted a little more. I was in mid-scoot when something hit me in the back of the ankles and I almost toppled off the ledge of the hotel. I turned my head to the side as much as I dared and glared at Pip.

"Would you keep your tail under control?" I hissed. "It's going to knock me off this building. Then you'll have to get Archie to come squeegee my ass off the pavement. Ain't nobody got time for that."

It may be my favorite new slang term. Maybe not new, but totally new to me.

"Sorry," she apologized. "It kind of has a mind of its own sometimes."

She struggled to catch her tail and finally grabbed hold, then stuffed it under her coat. It writhed around, and I anticipated it would burst out like an alien any second.

"You need to try. As long as Archie is working on his new rune and you don't have the one making you look at least partially human, you don't have anything to hold it back," I told her.

Pip gave a firm nod and held her arm across her tail.

I hoped it didn't have another sudden burst of movement that might fling the young lizard girl off the side of the building. As it was, our ability to balance on the narrow ledge was tenuous at best. We didn't need dangling to make it harder.

This might not have been the best plan I'd ever had. But it was what we were working with, so I would make the most of it. We kept moving along toward the balcony I was pretty sure was attached to the Russian Ambassador's suite. Pip and I scoped out the hotel where the Ambassador was staying, and it was no surprise the place was on heavy surveillance.

Security crawled around everywhere, making it impossible for us to walk through the front door and head up to his suite. That's what led to the brilliant idea of scaling the building and making our way through the balcony door. We only needed to get in and talk to him.

Unfortunately, that didn't look too promising. Now that we were getting closer to the balcony, I could see through the glass doors and noticed movement. Security guards were posted right inside. There was no way we would be able to get in without a bang. It was a wonder no news outlets had shown up yet to chronicle our death-defying climb. They were probably all distracted by the summit. Or maybe we were lucky enough for someone to have caused a massive multi-car pileup and all the cameras were there. Whatever it was, I'd take it.

Admitting defeat on the Spiderman front, Pip and I

made our way cautiously back across the ledge and onto the fire escape we used to get up there in the first place. We scrambled down and landed almost completely on our feet.

"We'll figure something out," she assured me, obviously seeing the look of disappointment on my face.

"I know," I told her. "Just have to think of what."

It was only the two of us at the moment. Archie was thigh-deep in the creation of a new rune for the next step of our larger plan, and Dog was off hunting down our other target while Ally drove around in the van, waiting for Pip and me to be ready. As we made our way back up toward the front of the hotel, I glanced over at Pip. I expected her to look as disappointed, but she was still determined, ready to keep moving ahead. I couldn't help but smile.

"Thank you for saving me," I told her.

She looked at me with an almost shocked expression, then shook her head.

"I barely did anything. No, that's not totally true. I got my ass kicked," Pip said.

I laughed. "Okay, that might be true. But you were there, and you tried, and I appreciate it. You might feel like you didn't do much, but it genuinely helped."

"It feels like I can't do much. I wish I could make a difference during fights. Not simply throw myself at people and throw them off long enough for one of you to come in and do the fighting," she lamented.

"Hey, don't underestimate the value of distraction. Throwing people off their groove and taking advantage of it has done me really well over the years. Remind me sometime to tell you about the night I escaped from the Deep, and how Splinter helped me with the Ogre," I said.

"Splinter?" She sounded surprised.

"Yep." I nodded.

"Splinter? You mean your bristly winged rat thing? The one who is currently hiding with Ally because you were afraid he would faint and fall off the building?" she asked.

"That's the one. He's small and can be an absolute pansy, but he has swooped in and saved my skin more times than I can count. Everybody has a role, but if you're determined to learn how to fight, I can give you a few pointers," I offered.

Pip looked at me with widened eyes and a huge smile.

"Really? You would do that for me?"

I laughed. "Of course, I would. Why wouldn't I?"

"Because I stowed away in your van, gave you something else to worry about during the fight, and almost knocked you off the side of a building?"

"Incidentals. Come on. We have some time 'til Ally gets in place. Knowing her, she's driving the wrong way up a one-way street. Let's try a couple things. We can keep working on it later," I said.

We stopped in the alley, and I sent my mind back in time to the earliest days I spent in the Deep. Solon threw me headlong into my training in those days, not giving me any wiggle room for excuses. When I didn't pick up the skills he tried to teach me, we trained harder.

We went through the same things over and over again until I knew them, and it wasn't uncommon for me to leave our sessions bruised and battered all to hell, but with one more little ability tucked in my pocket. Now it was time for the grasshopper to become the grass...or something.

A few minutes into our training, Pip's eyes snapped over to the side and she reached out for me. I was in mid-spin, about to teach her a kick that evolved from my early flailing days and almost caught her right in the head. I managed to stop and leaned toward her.

"What is it?".

"Look." She pointed at the back of the building where a figure walked out. "Don't we know him?"

I looked closer, and my heart jumped.

"That's the Ambassador's assistant." I paused for a second to let a plan form. Then I started toward the well-dressed man. "That will work. I'll distract him. Call Ally and have her come around the back, then come help me. We have to get him in the van."

"On it."

I rushed up behind the assistant, trying to decide what to say to him. "Hey!" burst out of me before I could think of anything else.

He turned to face me.

"Hello," he greeted me cautiously while his eyes darted around like he was looking for any of the security guards who might have covered him.

None were around. Score.

"So," I started, then caught up and stepped in front of him so he would have to turn around again. "How's the summit going?"

"Are you a reporter?" He spoke in a thick accent.

I forced a laugh far bigger than would be justified by that comment.

"No. Not a reporter. Simply a concerned citizen being…concerned." I swung my arms, trying to look breezy and carefree.

He might have said something else, but I would never know what it was. A slight buzzing sound followed by a gurgle and widening eyes preceded the assistant falling face-first onto the ground. And now I was a touch more concerned.

"Oops."

I turned to look at Pip, who had one hand in the taser glove and was looking down at the man sprawled on the ground. A second later, the van screeched up to the narrow road at the back of the hotel. Ally rolled down the passenger window and gestured at us to hurry up. Pip and I tucked our arms under the assistant's and half-carried, half-dragged him to the van. I opened the door and stuffed him inside.

"Sorry," I said. "This is for the greater good."

CHAPTER TWENTY-SIX

Pip and I scrambled up into the cramped van that made me miss the pimped-out ride we still hadn't named back home and slammed the door closed. It had barely latched when Ally took off again. I crawled over the assistant and yanked him farther into the space, then climbed up on the seat.

I heard an exasperated sound from the back of the van. I didn't see anybody when I first glanced back, but then a hand came up and clamped down on the edge of the furthest back seat. He climbed his way up and righted himself as he clenched a jar in one hand.

"Seriously, Ally. You need to give me more of a heads-up than that when you take off," Archie complained.

"Well, I'm sorry, but time is of the essence right now," Ally told him from behind the wheel.

From a pack beside him, Archie produced a syringe, which he summarily stuck in the arm of the ambassador's assistant and drew out some of his blood. After wiping the surface with a wet-napkin, he applied a band-aid and opened the jar. We turned a corner, and the vehicle went over something in the road. The bump made Archie squirt a small stream of the blood into the air, where it stuck on the top of the van.

"I won't be able to finish this rune if you send my supplies flying all over the place," Archie snapped.

Ally glared at him in the rearview mirror. "I'm doing the best I can. Do you want to come up here and do the driving, too?"

Archie didn't say anything else, only grumbled as he went back to work, depositing the blood into the jar and tightening the lid. He twisted around and used different ingredients to build the rune he was modifying, and eventually dipped it into the blood. A few minutes later, Ally turned a corner and pulled off the main road.

Not being out in the open made it easier for Archie to continue his work without risking others seeing us or Ally flinging it across the van. I stared at the unconscious assistant, contemplating our plan until I heard Archie make a sound that could be an acknowledgment. I looked over at him and saw him examining the rune.

"Is it finished?" I asked.

The rune looked like a pocket watch. Archie opened it, released the clasp that held the glass in place, and turned the minute hand around a full rotation. In an instant, he changed into a replica of the Ambassador's assistant.

"Holy shit," Ally gasped.

"Yeah," I agreed, glancing down at the unconscious man on the floor. "You look exactly like him. That's crazy." The effect of the rune flickered slightly, and suddenly the image of the assistant had Archie's hair. "Well. You almost look exactly like him."

Archie let out another sigh and tapped on the pocket watch. Inside was the rune Pip used in the airport to look as close to human as she could manage. Archie had been working on modifying it so it wouldn't simply make the user look human, but look like a specific human. It was a brilliant part of the plan—if it worked. If it didn't, we had Franken-people walking around, and that wouldn't be good for anyone.

"Give me a minute and let me tweak a couple things. It's still a little spotty, but it will work. Having the blood of the subject we're trying to emulate helps a lot."

"Make it as good as you can," I said. "If I'm going to impersonate this guy, I can't have it glitching on me. I might not know about all the advancements that have happened over the last ten years, but I'm pretty sure instant cosmetic surgery hasn't been invented yet."

"Nope, but drive-thru service is coming disturbingly close," Ally told me.

Her voice sounded ominous, and I could only imagine what news story she wrote that went into that comment. While Archie continued to tweak the rune, I decided I might as well keep going with the plan. I got down on the floor and flipped the assistant over so I could access his pockets. After fishing around in them, I pulled out his wallet and phone. I handed them to Ally with a hint of uncertainty.

"Are you sure about this? You're sure this will work?"

She nodded enthusiastically. "It's genius. We'll use the Shapeshifter's tactics against her. It's been working out pretty fantastically for her, and she's going around pretending to be an extremely public figure right in the middle of a peace summit. I think Ambassador's assistant will be easier than world leader."

"If I can pull it off," I modified.

"You'll be fine. Archie will get the rune working and you'll look just like this guy. I'm going to find out as much as I can about him so I can feed you intel. You don't have to keep it going for long," she reassured me.

I nodded as Ally's phone rang. She picked it up and made a few acknowledging sounds, then hung up.

"What was that?" I asked.

"Dog. He found her." Her eyes locked on mine for a second.

I immediately reached behind the seat to where Archie had stashed the weapons. Yanking the crossbow up with me, I checked it to make sure it was still in good condition.

"Where?" I asked.

"Here." Ally ripped a piece of paper from a notebook and scribbled something on it. "This is where to meet him."

"Perfect." I read over the address a few times to try to commit it to memory.

The pocket on the back of Ally's seat shifted and rolled, then Splinter wriggled his way out. He held a cheese doodle in his mouth as he scampered to me and hopped in my lap. I smiled and took the snack from him, then popped it in my mouth.

"Still so gross," Ally muttered, but I ignored her.

"Thank you, buddy. I've missed you recently. Want to come along with me this time?" I asked.

He crawled into my pocket and smooshed himself into the corner like he was trying to be inconspicuous. I patted the pocket affectionately.

"I want to go." Pip moved to the edge of the seat like she was readying to get up.

I shook my head. "No. Stay here with Ally and Archie."

"The toilet brush gets to go, but I can't?" Her voice bordered on whining.

"Splinter stays in my pocket most of the time. Besides, he's seen more combat than you have in your life. Hopefully, that's not what this comes down to. Hopefully, I'll go meet up with Dog, it will be smooth and easy, and it will be done," I explained.

"Just like that," Ally agreed.

"Yep. Remember, Pip. You know the plan. We have to follow it if we're all going to stay safe." I thought of something and smiled at her while leaning a little closer. "And if you stay here, you can watch Archie work on the rune."

Her face lit up, and she slid over toward Archie.

"Don't touch *anything*," the Philosopher grumbled.

"All right." I carefully climbed my way over the assistant. "Keep the assistant warm for me. I'll be back."

I opened the door and dropped out of the van.

"You need to hurry," Ally said. "The Ambassador will get suspicious if his assistant is gone too long. We don't want his security detail coming after us. Especially since I'm pretty sure there are surveillance cameras behind the hotel, and it won't be long before they see the two of you taking this dude down." She suddenly grinned and waved cheerfully. "Okay. Good luck! Off to save the world!"

No pressure.

Strolling around carrying a crossbow wasn't on my list of the top most subtle things I've ever done in my life, but it wouldn't fit under my jacket, so I didn't have much choice. Fortunately, it was still dark and there weren't many people out and about. The very few I saw didn't pay attention to me as I oriented myself and made my way toward the meeting spot to find Dog.

As I approached, I hoped the little map I was using was wrong. Then I saw the unmistakable figure standing several yards ahead of me, his back to me and his silhouette dark against the water. It was Dog. Dog waiting for me at a harbor.

I let out a sigh and reached for my radio to call Ally.

"Hello?" her voice crackled over the line.

"If I end up in the water again, I'll be pissed. I don't think Splinter will recover too quick, either."

"I'm sorry," she apologized.

"Well, you will be if he decides he wants you to cuddle

him and feed him chicken noodle soup to warm up," I warned.

I disconnected before she could say anything else. Mostly because Splinter had never had chicken noodle soup and I didn't know if he would have a taste for it. But the image of him wrapped in a blanket with a heating pad on his head and Ally having to pour tiny spoonfuls of broth into his mouth made me warm and fuzzy inside.

I looked around and saw lots of shipping containers and not a lot of people. We were talking prime horror movie real estate here. Maybe psychological thriller. Either way, I didn't think this would be a nice relaxing visit to the waterfront.

Dog turned to look over his shoulder at me as I approached. He turned the rest of the way around, and the tiniest hint of light on the horizon from the sun preparing to come up drew his features out of the darkness of his face. I fought the urge to hug him. But it felt like a hug moment.

"I'm glad you called. There isn't a lot of time. The sun will rise soon," I said.

I wasn't entirely sure all those pieces went together in the same thought, but they're what came out of my mouth. Being around Dog made making words harder recently.

"I know. Come on," he agreed. Oh, good. It did make sense. "I tracked the Shapeshifter's scent here." He looked down at my hands. "Nice crossbow. Steal it from Archie?"

"I didn't steal it. I borrowed it. This might not be a smooth experience, and I don't want to be caught off-guard. The last weapon Archie made for me almost blew me up, but he made this for himself, so I figured it had a better chance of not blowing my fingers off. The bolts are electrified through magic. It's pretty neat. Not only does it pierce the skin like a normal arrow, but then it gives them a helluva shock."

"Like a taser?"

"Yeah. But cooler. On account of it being a crossbow." I glanced at the weapon and back up at him. "Apparently, the bolts' explosive effects are connected to range."

Dog smiled. "Archie can't keep the boom up over a long distance?" I shrugged. "You could have brought the awesome axe." His eyes slid over to me, then back ahead of him.

"I could have. But I'm switching things up. Staying unpredictable," I bluffed.

"Well, if there is one word I would use to describe you, Sara Slick, that is it," he told me.

The heat on my cheeks returned, and I pulled my eyes away from him.

"Where are we going, exactly?" I asked.

He gestured at the shipping containers as we started walking toward their looming shapes.

"Right there." He pointed to the area. "It's where I tracked her."

"Why here? What would the Shapeshifter want around here?" I asked.

"What are those containers?" he asked.

I looked at the wall of multicolored metal containers stacked on each other and scattered around the harbor.

"Um. Shipping containers?" I replied.

"And what are they for?" he led.

"Shipping?" I asked.

"And what else?" he asked, and I shook my head. "Storage. And that's what the Shapeshifter needs. Odds are, they've kept Cabot alive for information. They couldn't do away with her because if they did, they would lose any access to details they need to continue infiltrating the summit. She needs to be alive to tell them what to do and how to fit in, and probably information about the government and how it works so they can blend in and do the most damage."

"So the Shapeshifter stored her," I concluded. Dog nodded. "We need to free her."

"Then we need to find her," he said.

We walked along for a few more seconds in silence before I turned to him again.

"Thank you," I told him.

He glanced down at me. "What are you thanking me for?"

"For saving me." Heat splashed across my cheeks and I swallowed hard. "I mean, for helping us."

Dog made a slight grunting sound and his lips curled up into something that might have been a smile.

"It feels good," he confessed.

"It does?" I asked.

He met my eyes again, and my heart jumped slightly.

"I've spent so much of my life consumed by hate. It was a part of me, something that defined who I was and almost everything I did. There wasn't a single day of my life that I didn't have rage inside me. I didn't connect to anyone or even want to. I always distrusted and disliked people on sight because I figured it was only a matter of time before they did something that gave me a reason to feel that way about them," he admitted.

"So, you got a head start," I said.

"You can say that. This is different. It feels good to do something to help others," he told me. "To work with others."

"Well, I know I for one am glad to have you as part of our team. I'm glad to have met you." I hazarded only a glance toward him.

"You are?" he asked cautiously.

I nodded, and he took a step that brought us closer so the sides of our bodies barely brushed against each other. But it didn't last for long. Seconds later, dawn broke, and when I glanced away from the new rays of sunlight at Dog, the handsome man was gone. In his place was the massive shaggy black dog with a dark intensity in his eyes.

A touch of sadness pulled on my heart. This was the form I'd originally met him in, but there was always a little disappointment when he changed from the man I could talk to and connect to more strongly to the huge animal.

Dog wriggled out of his human clothes, turned and trotted away from me. I tucked his garments into a bag, then followed close behind him, knowing his animal form had a stronger sense of smell and would be better able to track the Senator now that we were close. The seemingly never-ending assortment of shipping containers stretched as far as I could see and towered over my head.

There was no way we would find the one where the Shapeshifter kept Cabot by playing *Let's Make a Deal* and selecting lucky doors as we went. That might work out for the man dressed like a toaster or the woman who poured the entire contents of her junk drawer in her purse to prepare for the mini-game, but this was a touch more pressing.

"Do you know where you're going?" I asked. Dog snuffled. "Of course, you do."

We made our way past the neat lines of shipping containers and crates, but soon found ourselves at what looked like the entrance to a huge maze made out of the metal boxes. Perfect. Because the stacks of them weren't enough. Now we got to frolic through the labyrinth.

Which, actually, in other circumstances, would probably be fun. I was not above a good, mature game of hide and seek. Only, I would much rather be doing the hiding than the incredible amount of seeking I saw in my future.

Before we could go through the entrance into the maze of shipping containers, Dog stopped. He sniffed the ground and looked around, then moved to either side and continued to sniff. Coming back close to me, he hunched down nearer to the ground, his fur bristling as a low growl rumbled around in his chest and reverberated in his throat. He might not have been using words, but I knew exactly what he was saying. There was danger close by.

There was only one choice, only one thing we could do. We couldn't see anyone, but there was a heaviness in the air and in Dog's growl that said someone was here who wouldn't be happy to see us. It was treacherous to take one step further.

I tightened my grip on the crossbow and patted the pocket where Splinter still curled out of sight.

"Ready?" I murmured, and we headed forward into the maze.

CHAPTER TWENTY-EIGHT

While dipping through various parts of the maze, I realized how brave Dog was. He'd pushed his nose almost flat against the ground, and he walked blindly toward whatever danger was before us but did it willingly so he would encounter it first. I didn't want anything to happen to him, but part of me was thankful that for once I wasn't the one in the lead, first to get attacked. Knowing my luck, whoever was at the end of this maze would wait until we were both in and try to surprise us by attacking me from behind.

Darkness overtook us as we moved farther away from the streetlights and into the depth of the maze. I held tight to the crossbow, knowing I needed to keep my wits about me. I only had so many bolts, and they were exceptionally powerful. I didn't want to waste them. That left the glove, which I couldn't depend on, and my switchblade, along with hand-to-hand fighting and Dog, who was a weapon all to himself. Whatever was lying in wait would have a battle on their hands. The question was how quickly I would end it.

Dog whimpered. Not a fearful one, but to get my attention without barking. The early morning light was all but completely hidden by the maze, and I could barely make out the shadow of him sitting and looking at me. I stopped where I was and looked around quickly. No one was near.

"What is it?" I whispered.

Dog whined again, only this time he stood, and I heard the clicking of his nails on the concrete as he led me toward a corner. He stopped before he went around it, and I thought I figured it out. I had to choke back the desire to say "good boy" and instead, laid myself against the wall and tried to peer around it.

A dozen or so yards away, two vampires stood guard in front of a metal storage container. They looked like the lower level ones I'd met in the alley, although these seemed a little more put together. The ones in the alley were animalistic and vicious, but entirely organic and weak. Something about these said they were stronger, smarter, perhaps imbued with some dark power from their master.

Archie had said something about the longer a vampire was around, the stronger it got. These must have been around a long time because they looked like they were a lot more solid than the weak, frail-looking ones I'd met before. They looked nearly human—almost indistinguishable. Only their pale skin, red eyes, and fangs gave them away.

Before I could come up with a plan, Dog trotted out from behind me and walked directly up to them. Their backs were turned at first, and I tried waving frantically to get his attention before he presented himself to them like a Thanksgiving turkey. Instead, he stopped and turned to me, motioned with his head to indicate a darkness-shrouded path to the side, then swung back to the vampires. I got what he was saying, but damn if I didn't like it.

I took off from the shelter of the wall and ran as silently as possible to the shadows. Dog would get their attention for me, so I only had to put myself into position. I closed in as far as I could on the metal storage container, then accidentally kicked a bottle. The noise attracted the attention of the vampires, whose heads turned in my direction. Before they could get all the way, Dog barked and ran toward them, his tail wagging.

"What the hell? Get out of here, you stupid mutt," one of them said, apparently assuming the dog made the noise. Dog barked again, twice, and leaned down on his front paws, his tail still wagging. He was trying to get them to come pet him and give me the chance to get behind them, but they didn't seem like they were budging.

"Go on," one of them growled. "Get out of here before I kick the shit out of you."

"Why don't you kick the shit out of him anyway?" the other said, and they both laughed.

"I don't need to get bit," the first one said. "I'd rather rip the stupid thing's head off."

"Bet you can't," the second one said.

"Easy," the first one said, and stretched his arms. "Watch this. Come here, stupid little doggy."

Dog stayed where he was, and the vampire grimaced.

"Fine, I'll come to you, fucking mutt."

He took a few steps forward. As he did, I snuck as close to the second one as possible. When things happened, they would happen fast, and I needed to be in position. The first vampire put out his hand like he was going to pet Dog, and I tensed and flipped the switch on the glove. It was go time.

"Let me pet your stupid little he—" he began, then screamed as Dog clamped down on his hand. As the scream began, I reached under the second one's arm and shoved the gloved hand up to his throat. Even if the shock didn't happen, it would surprise the hell out of him to suddenly be choked by someone behind him.

I barely needed to think about what would come next as his body convulsed, then smoke appeared on his clothes and skin. I let go as he crumpled to the ground, finger marks burned into him and sparks shooting off his now rigid hair.

The first vampire was on the ground kicking at Dog, who jumped around and yanked his hand in his mouth. One foot landed hard on Dog's side and he skidded across the ground, letting go of the hand. I rushed over to them as the vampire got to his feet. He turned to me, bared his teeth, and hissed.

I swung the gloved fist and connected with his jaw, sending him barreling backward. The glove short-circuited and smoke billowed out of it, so I yanked it off and stuffed it in my jacket. This jerk would get the business the hard way.

I ran at him and tried to adjust my direction as he leapt up, dove over me, and rolled behind. His power gave him exceptional agility. Dog latched onto his ankle and shook, which gave me enough time to stop, spin, and charge him again. I reached him as he tried to leap up again after kicking Dog away hard. I grabbed him by the belt and yanked him back down. As his surprised face came into view, I threw my head forward and smashed his nose and mouth with the top of my head.

He swung at me and connected with my ribs as I shoved an elbow toward him, hit him in the nose, and sent him reeling backward. As he hit the ground, I pulled the switchblade out and jumped. Before he could roll out of the way, I landed hard on his stomach with my knees and buried the knife in his chest. I pushed it deep into him as his hands reached up and grabbed my throat. I held it there as he struggled, slowly losing strength as dark, almost brown blood pooled around him. Finally, he stopped struggling, and his arms fell by his sides. I relaxed, turned to Dog, and smiled.

"That was easy." I wiped the knife on my jeans. Rattling sounded from inside the container like someone was trying to open the door.

"Hello, is someone out there?" came a voice from inside.

"Hang in there, I'm trying to get you out," I shouted while looking through the vampire's clothes for a pair of keys. He had none, and I realized his buddy must have been the one with them. The door rattled again, and I turned toward it, meaning to reassure them I was coming as I walked toward the other fallen vampire when something rushed across my vision and sent me flying backward.

I landed hard on the ground and looked up. In the darkness, light barely illuminating his face, stood the assassin from before. He smiled and bared a set of terribly sharp teeth, then licked his lips. I reached for my knife and realized he had knocked it out of my hands, and now it was somewhere behind him. He walked toward me with a determined focus.

Well, shit.

CHAPTER TWENTY-NINE

I scrambled to my feet, only to get knocked back hard by a stinging kick to my stomach that simultaneously knocked the wind out of me and made me lose my footing. Dog leapt at him as I hit the ground, and the assassin swiped at him with the back of his hand. He connected hard and sent Dog flying into the shadows while yelping. Suddenly, he was in the air and diving at me. I rolled barely in time to avoid his foot, which stomped into the ground so hard it made a small crater.

He stomped again and again as I kept rolling, then finally got into a position to roll another direction and create some space between us. I barely caught my breath and made it to my feet before the assassin was in front of me, his eyes glowing white and his sharp jaw sticking out from the long hair covering his face. The gloved fingers on his outstretched hand reached for my throat, but I dodged and caught him hard in the cheek with a fist.

It was enough to make him stumble. I took advantage of the moment by rushing him, then landed a few more shots to his ribs and finally, an uppercut that should have knocked him into next week.

Instead, he took the shot on his chin, which forced it to rock back, then rolled into place again as if a rubber band controlled it. His expression didn't change. He still smiled like mad, and the grinning, terrible teeth—far too many teeth—shone in the random, dim light. His eyes glowed a bright white, like LED flashlights stuck in his skull, and there was silence for a moment.

"Well, this has been real, but I'm gonna…" I began, and turned to run. A powerful hand grabbed me by my back and tossed me over my head and careening to the ground.

"You will go *nowhere*. You will do *nothing*. Except die," the slithering, grumbling voice of the assassin said.

"Anybody ever tell you that you talk like an anime character?" I got out before another fist smashed into my jaw and I flew back into a chain-link fence.

From where I was, I could see the bag I brought that contained a couple of goodies Archie had stashed for me. I grabbed my crossbow, which I had dropped when the action got hot. If I could get a bolt and load it, then if worse came to worst, I could fire it, and this might end up being a somewhat fair fight. I stood and turned to dive in the bag's direction when I heard the assassin snap his fingers. I stopped cold.

In the distance, from where I buried the knife in his chest and emptied the goo that passed for his blood, the vampire goon sat up and turned his head toward me. His eyes now glowed orange. Beyond him, the Kentucky Fried goon also rose. His hair still stood on end, and his throat bore the marks from the glove.

My jaw dropped. I'd never seen anything I put down that hard get up. I'd also never seen anything I killed not only wake up, but also look *stronger*.

"Waste her," the assassin grumbled, and the goons pulled out what looked like Uzi machine guns from their jackets. A spray of bullets lit up the ground in front of me, and I dove to grab the bag before high-tailing it back the way I came.

I reloaded the crossbow while thanking every deity I could think of that Archie had given me one with an easy mechanism, then pointed it behind me. I didn't necessarily need it to hit anything, I only needed them to know I was firing back. I pulled the trigger, and a bolt shot out hard as the recoil jolted my arm.

The bolt exploded in a trash can behind me and sent it barreling through the air and into one of the now-charging vampires. It flung him backward and into the storage container, and he sizzled as the trash can conducted the arrow's electricity, accidentally making it a larger weapon. I made a mental note that when I got through these guys, I still needed to help whoever was in there.

Dog was behind me, his feet pounding on the concrete as he kept pace while we sprinted back into the maze. I knew I could follow his senses and get back to the beginning, but he moved faster than me, and I quickly lost sight of him. Rather than wait for him to return, I took off on my own while trying to remember the maze, or at least find a way to create an advantage.

I headed deeper into the maze in a direction I didn't recognize, dipping and diving through various turns as I listened for the sound of gunshots behind me. I skidded to a halt at another blind turn and waited while trying to listen above the sound of my heartbeat in my ears.

Something was on the other side of the large shipping container. A couple of somethings. I heard them whispering to one another in the hissing, vile sound the other vampire goons used. I pulled the bag off my shoulder and searched as silently as possible to see how many crossbow bolts I had left.

I knew I wanted to conserve as many as possible, but knocking out two of these guys at once might be worth the shot. I took a bolt out and placed it in the divot, then pulled it back so the wire went taut. I exhaled a long slow breath and prepared to round the corner and get the drop on them.

I didn't get the chance.

As I got within feet of the corner, one of their heads popped out at me, surprising me so much I pulled the crossbow's hair-trigger and fired before I'd truly aimed. The bolt struck him in the center of his forehead, and his skull exploded. Brain matter flew into the air and blood splattered the wall of the shipping container. A piece of his scalp seemed to float down and land at my feet as I stared blankly at the place where his head used to be.

His body took a second before falling like its head's sudden removal shocked it, and when it landed on the ground, I noticed my jaw was moving. I had been screaming the letter U from the word "fuck" for several seconds. Eventually, the hard K sound tumbled from my lips, and I regained some measure of control over my mouth.

Another head popped out from behind the shipping

container. This one was looking down at the last head to try that tactic and was still dumb enough not to avoid repeating the mistake. Thankfully for him, I was still so taken aback that I hadn't reloaded the crossbow. The head turned to me and our eyes met, and we stared at one another for several seconds, both unsure of what to do next.

Then, with a sound like opening a soda bottle that someone had shaken for a few hours, the world returned to normal speed and normal thoughts. I scrambled for the next bolt, but he was already on me and tackled me before I could reach one.

We tumbled on the ground together, both jockeying for position before I planted my foot in his midsection and hoisted him up and over to land hard on his back. I rolled backward and pushed up until I was in a handstand, then crashed down knees first into his chest. I still had one weapon left I could use other than the bow, and I pulled it out while hoping it worked this time. I pulled the glove onto my hand and looked down into the gnashing face of the vampire.

"Eat this, blood breath," I shouted and flicked the glove on, then shoved it hard into his face. Electricity poured out of it, and soon the smell of burning flesh accompanied his screams.

I held it there, pushing hard down into him while moving my head away so I could try to escape being splattered by his blood, too. His arms thrashed and pushed, but my knees pinned him down at the shoulders, and he soon stopped moving. I took the glove away and looked down at the mangled mess I left.

His face was a puddle of goo and bones. A giant burning hole sat where his mouth had been, and where I had shoved the glove. Teeth, sharp as needles and broken into tiny pieces, scattered the ground around me. I sighed heavily as I sat back, turned the glove off, and thought I might get a second to rest.

A howl ripped through the air, and I snapped to my feet. It was Dog, and he was hurt—by the sound of it, badly.

CHAPTER THIRTY

I tore off back the way I came. Another howl pierced the air, and I pushed myself to run faster, blindly turning through the maze in his direction. Every turn I made pushed me deeper into the confusion. I spun around to the sounds of footsteps pounding behind me, but no one was there. Panic settled in my stomach as I tried to make sense of where I was in relation to the sounds and where I had been. Nothing clicked. The more I turned around corners, the more lost I felt, and the more I felt like I was running in circles.

Then it hit me. I didn't have to run through the maze if I could get on top of one of the large containers. I had practiced running up walls by bouncing along corners of concrete to climb up and away from dangerous monsters plenty of times in The Deep. If I could find a solid corner of walls, I could probably get to the top and see where I was and how to get to Dog. I rounded one more corner and found what I was looking for.

I pushed myself to my top running speed, kicked out

with one foot, and threw my body weight at one side of the metal wall, bouncing off and repeating it on the other. I had at least four good bounces before the momentum would drop, and I needed to get my fingers on the top of the large shipping container before that happened. The third bounce sent me lower than I thought it would. I cried out as I kicked one last time and moved away from the corner, but barely got the tips of my fingers on the top.

I hung there for a second, then shifted my hands so I had the palms over the edge. A swing toward the corner allowed me to run my feet up the wall, then flip over and land inches away from the edge on top of the container. I sat back and let my heart settle for a moment before checking the crossbow. There were three bolts left. It would have to do. Another howl rattled in my bones, and I could only imagine what the assassin and his goons were doing to Dog.

When I stood, the entire maze was visible from above. My container was one of the tallest, and I thanked whatever watched over me for that piece of luck. There were a few dead ends I could make out, and a clear path snaked back to the main container where the dim lights shone down on the one I hoped contained Cabot. Dog must have gone back there, because another sound, more like a whimper than a howl, came from that direction. I had to move, and quickly.

I took a running start and leapt from the top of one container down onto another. A small building like a security office was next, and I leapt up to grab its roof, then climbed over and ran across it to reach the next container.

It suddenly reminded me of all the crazy parkour

videos Ally and I watched the summer before they took me to the Deep. I wished like hell Ally could see me do this in a non-emergency situation so she could freak out about how cool it was. I silently promised myself that if I could get Dog out of here alive, I'd show her a few tricks when I got back to them.

The sound Dog was making broke my heart, and worse, it pissed me off. Someone hurting an animal was bad enough, but this sounded like torture. Whatever was happening sounded like more than someone defending themselves, it was yet another person trying to hurt him because they thought he was 'only an animal.'

I bounded across the top of another container and the clearing spread itself out below me. Dog huddled near the middle of the area. The assassin leaned over him with one long fingernail piercing his skin and turning it, so he ripped the open wound. My heart leapt into my throat at the thought of the pain Dog was in, but I had to steel myself. Another vampire stood at the entrance to the clearing below me. I judged the distance and jumped.

My knees hit the side of his head and neck as I torpedoed to the ground. It was enough to knock him down, and I scrambled on top of him, then repeatedly bashed him in the head with the butt of the crossbow until he gurgled his last breath. When he finally stopped moving, I turned toward the assassin. He still tortured Dog, not seeming to pay any attention to me. It gave me a second to load another bolt and aim. After adjusting for his methodical movements, I pulled the trigger.

The bolt flew with precision and hit directly in the center of the assassin's back. At this distance, the concussive behavior of the arrows wasn't nearly as explosive, but it knocked the crap out of him. It jammed into him with a whump sound, and he flew off his knees, then landed hard on his chest a few feet away. Dog quickly limped away while looking back at me with a pained face that made me all the madder. I loaded another bolt and waited.

The assassin stood and opened his mouth to say something as he turned, blood trickling down from his chin where it had scraped on the concrete. I fired. He barely got a sound out before the bolt hit him directly in the chest and he flew back, skidding on the ground while moaning in pain. That one got him good. I tore off after him, jumped, and landed knee-first on his stomach.

His hands reached up and grabbed me around the throat. I saw purple spots in my vision and knew I wouldn't last long with him choking me. I let go of the crossbow, jammed my fist into his face, and felt the bones in his cheek crunch under the force of the blow. His head rocked back and blood and spit flew out of his mouth, and his eyes dimmed a little. The grip on my throat lessened, and I reared back for another haymaker. It landed on his jaw, and I felt him loosen more. I was winning, and I had no intention of stopping.

"Nobody," I growled while slamming another shot into the side of his face, "hits," an elbow on the ear, "my friends!"

I raised both my hands and clasped them together, then brought them down hard on the bridge of his nose with an axe handle smash. The grip on my throat—once so vicelike I thought he would choke me out in a manner of seconds—disappeared, and his arm hit the ground weakly.

He was prone and hurt, and I could get any information out of him I wanted. But I wasn't ready for that.

The sound of Dog being hurt still rang in my ears. The image of the assassin bending over him and digging his nails into a wound with that terrible grin with all its teeth smiling down as he tortured him was too much. With a roar of frustration, anger, and exhaustion all piled up together, I rained down blows with both fists. I pounded him until I felt like my knuckles would break and his flesh tore off the bone.

His eyebrow was cut and bleeding, the plasma dripping down to meet the river running from his nose and the corner of his mouth. Finally, my blows slowed down, and I realized they were getting weaker. I grabbed him by the hair and yanked him up to look at me. The light in his eyes had almost completely faded, but red glowed in the center of them like an ember in a fire. He was still there. He could still talk.

"Now," I wiped the blood from my mouth with the back of my free hand, then clenched my fist once more, "I have some questions. And you will give me answers."

CHAPTER THIRTY-ONE

"Die wanting," the assassin spat at me, and I laid another elbow into his jaw. Nobody got snippy with me.

"I didn't say anything about wanting. I said I have some questions and you *will* give me answers. I didn't leave room for debate in that," I spat at him. "Who sent you after me?"

"Get fucked," he sputtered.

I reared back to lay another fist on him when I noticed Dog standing beside me. He was obviously hurt, but I could tell he felt better. More bitey. I nodded at him. Without a moment's hesitation, he clamped his jaw around the assassin's leg. The assassin shook it as hard as he could, but I adjusted my knee so it shoved down on his thigh. The assassin howled in pain.

I held up my hand to stop him. "Hold on, Dog. I think he has something to say."

"Get that damned dog off me," he yelled.

"Oh, you like to play rough?" I grabbed the last bolt from my bag, then picked up the crossbow, loaded it, and pointed it directly at his crotch. "I wonder how rough you like it."

The assassin's eyes bulged as he looked down at the crossbow hanging above his precious dangly bits. He might be imbued with otherworldly powers and abilities, but having his crotch explode into a million pieces wasn't likely something he could simply shake off.

"You know these bolts go pop? Magic is badass."

"You wouldn't," he pleaded, but one look in my eyes told him all he needed to know. Not only would I, but I *wanted* to.

"Oh, no?" I asked.

The assassin nodded weakly.

I looked the weapon up and down. "What *exactly* do you think this does at close range?"

There was a moment where the calculation set in, and I could almost imagine the terror going through his mind at the thought of his balls exploding. He swallowed hard, and the light in those glowing eyes dimmed further and deepened in red. I grinned.

"Fine." He gave up, his voice almost a croak as he forced the words out. "Fine. Hobbes hired me."

"That figures." I pushed the crossbow bolt into his crotch a little, which elicited a whimper. Even the undead had this weakness, it seemed. "Who the hell is Hobbes?"

There was another moment of silence as the assassin seemed to wrack his brain. Whether it was for an accurate description to tell me, or an elaborate lie, I didn't know. But hopefully I was giving him enough of the crazy eye that he wouldn't lie if he valued having all of his parts later in the day.

"I don't know," he pleaded.

I dug the crossbow bolt a little harder and Dog shook his leg a little more vigorously.

"I swear, I don't know," the assassin continued. "I never met him directly. I got communications from someone else who got it from someone else and so on. No one I know has seen Hobbes' face. We all do what he asks and get paid for it."

"Just so you know, I have no issue splattering every inch of your reproductive organs all over this place and leaving you that way."

"I don't want that at all," he half-croaked. Something about his voice was pitiful now. Almost human-like. I figured it was some kind of glamour vampires used to be less intimidating to people they planned on using. I wasn't falling for it.

"I think you're lying," I informed him as I jammed the bolt down hard. He clenched in pain, then stared back up at me again. The gleam in his eyes was gone. No more white, no more red, only a cold and distant silver, like whatever possessed his body was now leaving.

A crackle in my pocket startled me and I realized I had left the headset in there the whole time. I reached in, fished it out, and placed it in my ear.

"Hello? Hello?" I said into it to nothing but static.

Suddenly, the assassin violently rolled to his side, knocking me off and onto my back. His fist was in the air before I processed what happened and he caught me once on the jaw, hard. Dog barked behind him, and there was shuffling as the assassin tried to kick him away to no avail.

The assassin looked back at me, his mouth widening and exposing rows of sharp, terrible teeth.

His eyes glowed a dark purple with a red swirling core and mesmerized me. I felt myself losing the will to fight back and only wanted to stare into those eyes. He came closer, and a small voice in my mind screamed that I had to do something fast.

Dog barked again, this time right next to my ear. I snapped back to reality, yanked up the crossbow, and fired. The effect on the assassin was twofold. First, he lifted off the ground several feet as the bolt picked him up. Then he exploded, starting in his chest where the bolt hit him, and ripped parts of him off and flung them across the open area.

Hot, black blood rained down on the concrete, but since the bolt was so intense, it went everywhere instead of only on me. After a few seconds of blinking at the sky where I saw him explode, I sat up, shocked to find I wasn't covered in recently deconstructed assassin.

Even if I had been, I probably wouldn't have cared much right then. Definitely later. That would have been a very long shower. But not right then. I was too focused on the mission that brought us to the harbor in the first place. I threw open the shipping container and saw Cabot lying on the cold metal floor. She looked a little rough, but that only further convinced me it was really her. I ran to her side and dropped to my knees to pull her up.

"Are you okay?"

She pulled away from me, her eyes wide. Damn. I'd spooked her.

"Who are you?" she demanded.

She sounded pretty tough for a woman who went through everything she did.

"Don't be afraid. I won't hurt you. We're here to help," I said.

"We?"

I looked behind me and remembered she saw a hulking black dog rather than the man I knew him to be.

"Me. I'm here to help. Come on." I reached for her hand and tried to pull her to her feet, but she pulled away again.

"What the hell is going on here?"

"I know this is a lot and you don't have any reason to trust me, but I highly recommend you do because if you don't, some seriously bad shit will go down. We don't have time to churn all the way through it right this second, but I can explain on the way." I gestured for her to follow me.

Some part of that sank in and she nodded, then let me help her up and guide her out of the shipping container. The world leader seemed fairly steady on her feet, all things considered, but I supported her as we hurried through the maze.

She gasped at the blood streaked across the ground and the bodies strewn in the corridors between the shipping containers. I barely noticed the carnage, but Cabot looked like she was losing her ability to keep walking forward. She squeezed her eyes closed and pressed her fingertips to them.

"I don't believe this. I don't believe any of this. I don't believe this is happening," she muttered.

My coat wiggled, and Splinter scrambled out of the pocket. He took his place on my shoulder and waited until the world leader moved her fingertips away and opened her eyes. She gasped again and took a slight step back, but Splinter smiled widely at her.

"See?" I asked. "Everything will be fine."

Whether she believed it or was so freaked out by everything happening that she didn't know what to do, Cabot nodded and continued to follow me. I got us through the maze, and when we stepped out and away from the shipping containers, Cabot drew a deep breath.

"I didn't think I'd ever get out of there," she confided.

Before I could say anything comforting or inspiring or any of the other things I would say if this was a movie of my life, my radio squawked. Cabot's eyes snapped to me like she thought I emitted the sound. She looked visibly relieved when I showed her the simple and familiar device.

"Slick? Are you there?" Ally said loudly through the radio.

"I'm here."

"Where the living hell have you been?" she snapped.

"So delightful to hear from you, too. I'm doing fine and freed Cabot safely, thank you for your concern." I rolled my eyes and a series of clicks and white noise came through. "What?"

"I've been trying to contact you for the last hour and a half," Ally shouted.

"I'm sorry. The reception must be bad here. And by here, I mean England."

"Slick, the summit is starting," she told me.

"Oh, shit," I muttered.

"What? What is it?" Cabot asked.

"The summit is starting," I told her, and her eyes went

wide. I started walking again. "We're hurrying back. Have the assistant ready."

"It's too late."

My heart jumped into my throat. "What do you mean it's too late?"

"The Ambassador was texting the assistant non-stop. We couldn't delay any longer." She let out a shuddering breath.

"What does that mean?" I demanded.

Ally drew in another breath. "Archie had to go in your place."

CHAPTER THIRTY-TWO

"Why, yes, I do love human foods. Particularly those I have to chew."

I shook my head and dropped my head into my hand.

"Dear lord, Archie, stop talking," I groaned.

"He can't," Ally pointed out. "They keep talking to him."

She stared at the radio in disbelief. Archie's voice coming through it had the same unnatural lilt as it did when he was trying to be human at the airport before our flight to London. This time, he didn't seem able to regulate his volume. Not only was he saying inane things, but sometimes each word in a sentence got louder and higher until he was almost shouting, then they tumbled down to close to a whisper.

We were all piled in the back of the van, cringing our way through the radio broadcast of the summit where Archie was doing his best human impersonation. Which meant it was a terrible human impersonation.

"Yes, I often envision my life in five years. I believe I will solve world hunger and live among the goats."

I looked at Cabot, who hadn't stopped staring at Pip. Her eyes moved along the lizard girl's green, scaly face and down to her tail draped over the seat beside her. Sometimes her mouth moved like she was going to say something about it, but she hadn't made any sounds yet. It was like the words formed themselves in her brain and made it to her mouth before she thought better of them and abandoned them.

Every few seconds, Pip looked back at her and smiled. Lord love her, she had no idea she was freaking Cabot the freak out.

"…only recently become familiar with profiteroles, I have not yet tried that variety. However, I can only assume they are as delicious as their vanilla and chocolate cream counterparts."

My attention snapped back to the radio, then to Ally.

"What? What did he say?" I pointed at the radio. "What was that?"

Ally shook her head. "Something about profiteroles."

"Is that a thing?" I asked.

"No. No, it is not." Her head didn't stop shaking, but her eyes squinted smaller and smaller the more he spoke.

"What was the question he was supposed to be answering?" I asked.

"His feelings on nuclear proliferation," Pip told me.

"Oh, lord."

"I don't even know what that is," she commented.

"Neither do I, but I'm sure it has nothing to do with cream puffs," I told her.

"Now, if you don't mind, I have a question for you," Archie's voice said through the radio.

"No. Oh, no, no, no." I shook my head. "*I* mind. I mind. We all mind."

"The somewhat limited knowledge I possessed of London before I came here as assistant to the Ambassador involved the phrase 'pip, pip, cheerio.' I was under the impression that was the widely accepted ritual when parting. Now, I have since learned it has nothing to do with Pip as I know her…"

"That's me! He mentioned *me*!" Pip gushed, and Ally gestured for her to quiet down so we could hear the rest of the train wreck.

"However, I'm still plagued by the question of the 'cheerio' portion. Was that inspired by the delightfully toasted oat breakfast cereal, or did the cereal come after?"

My head dropped back, and I pressed my hand over my eyes.

"This couldn't get worse." I moaned.

"Well, no. Let's not lose hope quite yet. I think Archie is holding his own. Possibly a little food-centric, but it's a good time for a snack. Everybody else there is probably hungry, too. Stay positive." Ally smiled at me, her eyes a little too wide.

I thought she was potentially reaching a little too far with the positivity efforts. We were listening to Archie's attempt at seeming human go rapidly downhill and there was nothing we could do about it. The least we could have done was give him more of a crash course in being human before we unleashed him on the world.

"Why did you let him go?" I asked Ally.

"He insisted. The Ambassador kept calling, and it was kind of tense in here. Archie said we were out of time and if we were going to do this, it needed to happen right then."

"But why didn't you go? He could have as easily taught you how to use the rune and you could have gone in my place," I suggested.

Ally shrugged while slowly shaking her head. "He said it had to be him, in case something went wrong with the rune." She looked back at the radio.

"Damn him. At least you know how to sound like a human during an interview rather than rambling about the fine nuances of the various flavors of M&M colors," I pointed out.

"You should have let me go," Cabot interjected. "None of you should be there. It should be up to me to fix this."

"What do you think you could have done?" Ally challenged.

"I could have explained things," Cabot told her. "If you let me go now, I can straighten all of this out and it doesn't have to get any worse."

"No." I shook my head. "Absolutely not. That's not an option."

"Why not? You said that at least Ally would have sounded like a human. That's not exactly a resounding endorsement. If you let me go, I can explain things to these people in a way they'll understand. I know what they're talking about. I can smooth it all over."

"No," I insisted. "You can't."

"Why not?" she repeated.

"No one would believe you," Ally pointed out. "If you walked into that place and told them not to worry about the rambling man in the strange outfit, he's only somebody derived from another realm who specializes in making objects that have magical powers so he doesn't do the whole speaking human thing terribly well, they would take you down. They would lock you up in a matter of seconds. And if you shut Archie up and successfully explained that whole situation, what would you tell them next? That a Shapeshifter abducted you, then made itself look exactly like you so it could infiltrate the peace summit?"

"I could start there," Cabot offered.

"And get tossed into a teeny little padded room where they stare at you through a small observation window in the door. It wouldn't go over well. And if they believed any of that, why should they trust you?" I pressed.

"What do you mean?"

"If you tell them a creature capable of looking and sounding like you abducted you, why would they trust that you weren't the Shapeshifter yourself? It could all be a ploy, pretending to be the real Senator while the one they've all been watching is the fake."

"But I *am* the real Senator, and the one they've all been watching really *is* the fake," Cabot pointed out.

"And how would they know that?" I prompted. "You could say that so they believe you and fall into complacency. Then you'd have them at your command and could continue with your devious plan."

Cabot paused for a few seconds.

"What?" she finally asked.

"Confusing, isn't it?" I sympathized. "Of course, they'd think you were the Shapeshifter if you came out and said you were the real you. That's exactly what the fake one would say."

"That's what the fake one *is* saying!" she exclaimed.

"That's the point," Ally reminded her. "You can't simply walk in there with those people and try to explain it all away. They aren't ready to hear that kind of truth. The reality we're dealing with right now is that the Shapeshifter has all the power here."

"So, what are we going to do?" Cabot asked. "Because I can't sit around here for much longer. There's too much at stake."

"There's only one play. We need to make a swap." I glanced at Ally, then looked back at Cabot with a sigh. "I told you I'd keep you safe. But that might mean pushing you toward danger."

The Senator looked resolved, ready for whatever was coming her way next. She had already survived captivity. She was prepared to handle whatever else I had for her. Or at least try.

"I don't really understand what's happening here, but if it means saving the world, then I'm in," she agreed.

"All right," I told her. "Let's do this."

CHAPTER THIRTY-THREE

"Are you sure about this?" Cabot asked as we approached the building where the summit was taking place.

The crowd of reporters and police created a thick wall of people around the building, all bustling and jostling around like none of them knew what was going on.

"Absolutely not." My steps didn't falter, but Cabot stopped in her tracks, and I had to go back to get her.

"Seriously?"

"Oh, don't be like that. It's only a figure of speech." Her expression didn't change, so I looped an arm through hers to encourage her to come with me. "Come on. It will be fine."

I'd done my best to take as much of Ally's optimism with me as I could when Cabot and I left the van. That's pretty much all I had to go on at the moment. A hunch, having no real other option, and a lot of optimism. So far, it was working out for me. We'd only now gotten to the summit, but I would take it one step at a time.

"What's wrong?" Speaking of Ally, her voice came

through the earpiece I wore under my hat. I pressed it deeper into my ear and tried to look inconspicuous.

"Everything's fine. We're having a pep talk before we head inside."

"All right. Well, I'm here. Let me know if you have any trouble or need anything."

"Will do," I confirmed.

Cabot finally let me pull her into walking toward the building again.

"You know these outfits won't work." She gestured at her clothes, then mine.

"What are you talking about? We look fabulous."

She turned and glared at me through the black fascinator that came down over most of her face from the black velvet hat pinned to the top of her head with all her hair stuffed into it. My giant sunglasses and floppy red hat had a certain *Carmen Sandiego* vibe to them, but we went with classy for her.

"I look like a woman at the Kentucky Derby celebrating getting her hands on her rich husband's estate after she murdered him," she described.

I blinked a few times. "You go right to dark places, don't you?"

"After what I've been through, it's kind of hard not to," Cabot pointed out.

I scoffed and shook my head, then pulled the collar of my trench coat up higher around my neck to conceal my face more.

"Girl, let's not play the 'my captivity was worse than yours' game. You won't win. But I get it. Trust me, though. We can do this," I encouraged.

"Are you sure about it now?"

"Still not one hundred percent. But I think that's a good thing." I nodded.

"How do you figure?"

"If you're one hundred percent certain about something, you don't really have any reason to work too hard for it. It's already being handed to you, so there's nothing to strive for. You go about your life, la-di-da, and wait for things to fall into place around you. Knock a few percentage points off that certainty factor, though, and you start putting real effort into things. You don't get complacent. Not knowing what will happen next keeps you on your toes." I glanced at her and saw she didn't look as concerned. She still was, but now slightly more confident.

"All right. I'll go with you on that one. You might be mostly full of shit, but at least you're going somewhere with it."

"See? That's the spirit," I praised.

"And when the dawn of the new era of peace is upon us, we will notice it, for we will no longer be sleeping. It won't be night anymore. We'll all be up."

Archie's voice came through the headset, and I shook my head.

"There he goes again." I let my head fall back in exasperation.

"Will he ever stop talking?" Cabot asked.

"Not as long as people keep talking to him." I lifted my head. "Archie isn't good at acting like a human, but one thing he clings very hard to is social contracts. Or what he thinks are social contracts. Or what he thinks people think are social contracts. Essentially, if someone talks in his general direction, he'll keep answering. Unless it's one of us. He'll ignore us with no problem."

"Well, that's reassuring," Cabot grumbled.

"I blame the fact that he's impersonating such a good-looking Russian," Ally chimed in. "These Brits are fascinated by him. Maybe they'll chock up his weirdness to translation errors?"

I pressed the earpiece into my ear again and slightly tilted my mouth so I could respond. "There's that positivity again. Is Dog doing ok?"

"You have to start calling him something else," she told me.

A growl behind her was as good as him saying no.

"I'll take that as a yes, he's fine." I glanced at Cabot and nodded.

"Yes, he is, and he and Pip are watching me quite closely. I feel like I might be the one they suspect of trying to take over the world." She sounded distinctly displeased by this prospect.

She was exaggerating. At least, I hoped she was. Ally was manning the comms during this mission, while Pip and Dog manned her. It was their job to make sure she was well-protected in case Hobbes had any more surreptitious goons lying around being sneaky.

I put nothing past him. After the whole Shapeshifter situation came to light, I was even more on guard. Hobbes could have hidden his minions anywhere and waited for us to stumble across them, like the Easter egg hunt from hell.

Getting Pip to stay behind and be part of the nerve center wasn't the smoothest aspect of leaving. She wanted to come with us and prove she could be valuable to the group. She even cited the fighting techniques I taught her in the alley beside the hotel and said she was completely prepared to take on anybody who might come her way.

She had a crazy idea that involved scaling the scaffolding on the other side of the building that was shockingly well-thought-out, but for now, this was what I felt was best for her and the mission at hand.

I did my best to tell her she was woefully unprepared for actual combat if it came down to it without using hurtful words, but subtlety wasn't the lizard girl's strong point. She kept insisting she come along, saying Dog was plenty of protection for Ally and we could use extra hands.

And an extra tail. Not happening. Especially with Archie in possession of the rune that was the only thing making Pip blend in as much as she ever did. There was no way we would bring her along with us into a crowd of thousands of unsuspecting humans. There was already enough potential for them to deal with some serious, life-altering stuff in the near future. We didn't need to add a tiny Godzilla sighting to it.

I'd handed her the axe I took from Bentham and Thrash and told her it was her special job to protect the van. It made us leaving a little easier for her, Ally be damned. Nobody would get near that van without getting chopped between the eyes.

"Well, behave yourself. Unless you see Hobbes. Then don't," I told her. "I'll check in with you later."

Cabot and I made our way further into the crowd, inching our way toward the building. We got an assortment of strange looks I'd expected, but I hadn't prepared for the several layers of security we had to get through. We successfully snuck around the first few guards we encountered, but finally ended up stopped before reaching the door.

"No admittance," the guard grunted.

"We need to get in there," I told him.

He shook his head. "No one goes in there without authorization. Strict policy."

"We have authorization. We are definitely authorized," I insisted.

"Who are you?" he demanded.

"Caterers," I replied after a few stumbling seconds. "We received a specific request and are here to make an emergency batch of profiteroles."

He stared at me for several seconds but must have heard Archie's rambling earlier, because he stepped aside and let us through.

"What the hell kind of excuse was that?" Cabot asked when we were far enough away the guard wouldn't hear us.

"Archie trying to talk about them made me hungry, and I can't stop thinking about them. We need to make some. I'm sure cream puffs exist in England. Right?"

"I'm pretty sure they do," she confirmed.

But the next guard we encountered wasn't sure about anything. He stayed absolutely still in front of the door, his arms crossed over his broad chest like he was channeling his lifelong dream to be a bouncer.

"We need to pass through," I told him. "Urgent pastry situation."

"No one passes." He held out an arm, so I bounced off it when I tried to walk by.

"All right, Gandalf," I muttered. "No need to get all upset, but we need to get in."

"Is there a problem here?" Another security guard walked up and eyed both of us. Playing an incognito pastry chef wouldn't get us out of this one. A second later, Cabot flung off her hat and glared at them.

"Yes, there is. The problem here is that I'm expected at the summit and you people are too busy flexing your muscles to make sure I get inside safely. Do you realize I'm standing out here in the open?" she said angrily.

"Um," one guard started. "I… Um…"

He looked at the other, obviously confused.

"Senator Cabot, I'm so sorry. I thought you were already inside. I didn't realize it was you." He fell all over himself while trying to save face.

"Clearly. Because if you did, you would know how much danger it could put me in to force me to remove my cover this way. Do you realize the kinds of people who exist in this world today?" she demanded.

"I'm so sorry," the first guard apologized. "We would never intentionally endanger you. Please, go right in. Do you need anything else? Can we escort you to the main room?"

A hint of panic jumped up inside me. We definitely didn't need our new friends coming with us through the summit. If we ran into carbon copy, Cabot edition, this would get awkward really fast.

"No. I think you've done quite enough," she dismissed.

The guards opened the door, and we hurried inside.

CHAPTER THIRTY-FOUR

"That was damn impressive," I complimented Cabot as we hurried down a hallway.

"Yeah, well, one of those things you learn when you're a representative is how to get your way when you need to. You have to know how to talk to people," she advised.

"According to the widely respected and accepted oral traditions of the Appalachian people, 'the green grass grew all around, all around, the green grass grew all around that hole.' Now, as I understand it, there was also a tree in that hole. So, does that preclude it from being a hole? When does a hole being filled with something else stop being a hole and become the ground?"

I'd been so wrapped up in trying to get into the building that I had stopped paying much attention to what was coming through the earpiece. If I didn't hear Ally's voice, I figured it probably wasn't important. And I was right.

"Can you teach him to do that?" I gestured toward my earpiece.

Cabot laughed. "I think he'll need more work than I would ever have time for."

"Fair enough." I looked around. "Where are we going?"

"There's a lounge right around the corner. A green room. It's for the people involved in the summit, so they aren't always out in front of the audiences and cameras and stuff," she explained.

"That's nice of the organizers to set that up for you guys," I commented.

"It is. Which is why I'm fairly certain that's where everyone is right now. Show me a place with no press, and I'll show you a bunch of tired world representatives." She nodded knowingly.

"That doesn't sound like a fun game."

We rounded the corner and found another crowd. Fortunately, they didn't seem invested in stopping us, and we moved past them and through a door with nothing more than a sign on it declaring the space Private.

The door led us into the back of what looked like a small ballroom made smaller with a movable wall pulled into place across it. This created enough space for the people inside to mill around, but not so much that it seemed cavernous compared to the relatively small group.

"Look," Cabot whispered as she elbowed me slightly and nodded ahead of us.

The people inside the room had created several small groups with some milling around from cluster to cluster like they couldn't find one where they stuck. Ahead of us, the Senator sat in a chair with a drink in one hand and a stiff expression on her face.

Her face was Cabot's face. I felt the woman stiffen

beside me and knew she was trying to wrap her head around seeing herself across the room. The Shapeshifter muttered something to the person beside her, but her eyes —Cabot's borrowed eyes—swept back and forth like she was keeping track of her surroundings.

It wasn't only the representatives in the room. Several members of the security force stood out, making it seem less likely we could snag the Shapeshifter and run. I eyed Archie and returned Cabot's elbowing to point him out.

"Let's get closer to him," I whispered.

We tried to act normal and phase ourselves into the gathering. Cabot put her hat back on to avoid startling the others who might notice she'd duplicated herself, and we walked a slightly weaving pattern through the space. Archie's eyes flashed our way, but he made no acknowledgment of us standing there. I examined a silver tray of snacks sitting among many others on a long table and selected what looked like a little piece of beef rolled up on a tiny slice of toast.

I popped the entire thing in my mouth and Cabot looked at me with an expression that was a mixture of disgust and amusement.

"How is it?" she asked.

"Good." I shrugged. "It's no street taco or anything, but I could take down a few of these."

"I'm so hungry," she groaned.

"Then eat one," I told her. "Remember, we're trying to blend in."

"Yeah, you're the epitome of inconspicuous right now." She picked up one of the little pieces of toast and narrowed her eyes at my glasses. "Can you see through those things?"

"I can." Then I noticed she was picking her way around the edge of the bread rather than simply eating it. "Oh, go for it."

She shrugged and shoved the entire thing in her mouth. It was almost as impressive as her stance against the security guards.

"I've always said, philosophy is for the birds. And two birds, as you know, are always with you if you believe."

My eyes slid over to Archie. He'd raised his voice slightly and was still staring at the man standing across from him.

"Great. He's run out of logical word combinations and now loose words will start tumbling out of his mouth," I said.

"Well, yes. That is an interesting insight," the man struggled to reply.

Archie gave an over-exaggerated nod.

"It is. Like I said, philosophy is for the birds. And two birds are always with you."

"Yes. I heard you." The man glanced at the people around him like he needed to confirm the others heard the same thing he did.

"Two philosophy birds. With you. Right now," Archie emphasized.

"What in the living hell is he talking about?" Cabot asked.

"Ally, do you hear this?" I asked. "I think Archie's broken."

"It's code," Ally told me through the earpiece. "He's trying to warn you about something."

Cabot and I immediately went on the defensive and looked around, trying to identify the threat.

"What is it? What could he be warning us about?" Cabot asked.

I turned, and my chest tightened. "Them. That's Bentham and Thrash, agents of the Philosopher's Guild. And bad, bad birdies."

I still remembered the way Thrash looked as he took the axe from Bentham—almost gleeful to do the job.

Cabot drew in a breath, then looked at the security guards standing close by the Shapeshifter. She shook her head as her eyebrows knitted together in confusion.

"Who are they?" She nodded slightly toward the men. "I don't recognize them as members of my security team."

"That's because they're probably more of Hobbes's goons." I turned my mouth to send my voice to the receiver to Ally. "Ally, tell Pip and Dog to be ready. We might need backup."

"What's going on?" Ally asked.

"Bentham and Thrash are here. Nothing's happened so far, but be ready," I warned.

Suddenly, Archie's face looked for a brief second like it melted. His features drooped low, then sprang back up to reposition themselves into the right face. Cabot and I exchange fast glances. Archie laughed and squished his fingertips into his cheeks like he was trying to make sure they stayed attached to his skull bones.

"Must be all the lights. They're so hot, they're making my makeup run." He patted at his face.

The people around him looked at him strangely.

"You aren't wearing any makeup," one pointed out.

Archie gasped as his face warped again, the rune glitching so it couldn't hold the illusion.

"I'm not! Should I be?" he asked.

Bentham looked at him more closely, her eyes narrowing with suspicion as she stepped closer to him. We didn't have much time.

It was now or never.

I reached into my pocket and pulled out Lights Out. Bentham's eyes snapped to me when she saw the weapon, but I didn't hesitate. I pointed the gun at the Shapeshifter and pulled the trigger, and everything went dark.

CHAPTER THIRTY-FIVE

Slow-motion mayhem happened all around me, and I ducked out of the way of any quick-reflexed reactions. Knowing Bentham and Thrash, there would be magic coming in my direction, and I needed to make sure I didn't get plugged before we could accomplish the mission.

My glasses flickered to life as I hit the floor, and I rolled under the long table in the room. Archie had been quite proud of these glasses, and it was one of the few creations he made that I was fairly certain wouldn't explode on my face. Or at least, I was over fifty percent sure. More than simple night vision glasses, these could detect heat signatures and other abnormalities.

It was like the glasses from *They Live* were designed to look for Farsiders. I suddenly had a real taste for a stick of bubblegum. Feet stumbled and ran and tripped around me as the volume level of the room rose and everything seemed to not only return to normal speed but suddenly go into fast-forward.

I waited for a moment, letting them stumble around

and try to find their bearings while I prepared to jump out and grab the Shapeshifter. As I was about to make my move, a blinding light stung my eyes, and I instinctively yanked off the glasses. The light disappeared, and darkness reigned again. A few seconds later, the light flashed once more and illuminated the room of pushing, shoving and confused people.

I glimpsed Bentham and Thrash behind Archie and making their way toward the wall where I stood. Then the light disappeared. It had to be an emergency light, which meant there was a backup generator somewhere that would kick the power back on any second. I didn't have much time.

While sitting under the table, I silently counted the seconds between the next two flashes and slammed the glasses back into place. If I could move when it was dark and close my eyes when the light flashed, I would operate opposite how everyone else could and move twice as fast.

I stood, counting under my breath as I looked around. Bentham and Thrash were closer now, stopped for the moment to wait for the flash of light. Archie had turned toward them, and I knew he was about to try something stupid to distract them. It gave me an opening.

My eyes slammed shut, and for a second, light filled out beyond my eyelids and the volume of the shouting increased. Someone tugged on my arm, and I violently shook them off before the light zapped out and I turned to face them. It was the Senator, wielding her big, angry-looking knife. So…not the Senator. Shapeshifter. I dodged the blade, balled up a fist and swung for the fences, but missed her jaw as she fell to the side.

Something tripped her in the darkness, and I reached down to grab her as something else behind me barreled into me. I tumbled to the ground in a mess of arms and legs and shouting. I recognized some of the colorful curses coming from one of the bodies tangled with mine.

"Dammit, Archie!" I yelled.

"Go, Slick. I got Thrash. Go," he yelled back as he struggled with the Guild Agent.

I got to my feet and looked for the Shapeshifter again, but she seemed to be missing. Somehow, in that moment of confusion, she slipped away. Panic gripped my stomach at the thought of all of this being for nothing when I noticed the Shapeshifter standing against the wall, trying to hide itself by wiggling behind a bookcase. I ran to it but only got a few steps before I had to shut my eyes once more.

When I opened them, my eyes focused directly on the Shapeshifter who now stared wide-eyed in my direction. She saw me and didn't know where to go. All I had to do was get to her before the lights flashed back on again. I took a step.

A flying body tackle immediately knocked me to the floor. Fists flew into my stomach, and hands tried to grab my arms to disable them. I kicked and wriggled, trying to get free as the person attacking me shouted. I instantly recognized the voice. It was Bentham.

"Stop resisting!" she shouted over the commotion of the room.

"Bentham, listen to me!" I shouted back.

Bentham wrapped one of my legs in hers and tried to lock in an arm bar. I grabbed her by the hair and yanked her backward enough to slam my forehead into hers. It was enough to loosen her grip, and I wiggled my leg under me and out of her hold. I heard a familiar sound, like an airplane fan roaring to life, and knew she was gearing up for a magical blast.

A faint blue glow swirled in the darkness, and I dodged in time for it to sear past me, then bounce off the floor and away. My time was running out. I had to do something now. I reached up, grabbed Bentham in a headlock and popped my hips so I yanked her to the floor with me, my body pressing down on hers to apply pressure. As we hit the floor together, I snapped my eyes shut, and beyond them, the world filled with light.

"Get off me, Slick!" Bentham angrily shouted, and in the distance, I heard Thrash shouting similar things at Archie, who was still running interference. "You tried to kill Cabot! I saw you with a gun." She still struggled.

"No, I didn't," I argued while wrenching down on the headlock and trying to position her head so it angled toward the Shapeshifter. With the glasses, I could see the real Cabot making her way toward her in the darkness. In a moment, they would be face-to-face. When the lights came back on, Bentham needed to see it for herself. "Look!"

I timed it so she faced the two Cabots—one hiding behind a shelf and peeking out and the other making her way toward her, sliding across the wall in the darkness—as the lights flashed on. Bentham stopped struggling. I'd snapped my eyes shut, but two voices rose above the others in the distance and I recognized both of them as being Cabot's.

"What the…" Bentham muttered.

"See?" I shouted.

A loud whirring sound seemed to shake the building, and instead of blinking off, the light behind my eyelids only grew brighter. The electricity was trying to come back on, but it was flickering. I yanked off the glasses and looked across the room while squinting to get used to the sudden brightness. Against the wall, Cabot advanced on the Shapeshifter until she was right next to her, and suddenly, swung her fist and rammed it into the creature's jaw.

The Shapeshifter fell to a knee but then turned back, seeming to unhinge its jaw and hiss like a reptilian monster. She had her knife in hand again, and there was no doubt how she intended to use it.

"Let me go now, Slick," Bentham shouted from below me.

Against every instinct I had, I rolled away and let Bentham scramble to her feet. The lights flashed off and when they came back on again, Bentham was on her knees, her palms facing out as she prepared to use magic.

Several sudden, concussive rounds of magical shot filled the air, sounding for all the world like a revolver, and the chaos in the room quelled. Initial screams gave way to everyone ducking and dropping to the floor. The lights flashed off again as soon as the blasts ripped through the air, and seemed to be off for hours, but must have merely been seconds. When they returned once more, the real Cabot was still standing in her place and Bentham was still on her knees. But the Shapeshifter was gone.

"Slick," I heard whispered behind me. I turned to see Archie. He pointed at a door to his side.

I nodded and looked back at Bentham, who was wildly looking around for the Shapeshifter. For the moment, she seemed to have forgotten me. I had to take my chances while I could and get out of here and try to find where the shifter went.

Turning and ducking so I could blend into the crowd of people now rising from their crouched positions on the floor, I made my way to the door and exited, putting as much distance between me and the agents as possible.

CHAPTER THIRTY-SIX

As I ran out of the room, the sound of the pandemonium behind me was nearly deafening. Wherever the shifter had gone, it was likely the hell out of that room, and I needed to find it. The problem was, it could look like anyone, and this building was full of generic-looking glad-handers who smiled fake smiles and laughed too loudly at bad jokes. It was a Shapeshifter's paradise.

I bolted down the hall, then skidded to a stop at a fire exit. It seemed likely they would take off this way to get a floor of separation between us, so I dove through it and took the steps as quickly as possible. A sound like a door shutting below me told me I was on the right path, and I wished like hell for a railing I could slide down like when I was a kid. At the bottom of the steps was another door. I yanked it open and stopped to catch my breath at what I saw.

It was a lobby full of confused, scared diplomats and their pages. Everyone clustered in groups near the exit and milled around in a directionless shuffle that seemed simultaneously panicked and locked in indecision. The shifter could be any of them. Or none of them.

Shit.

I tore into the room and grabbed random people as I went, yanking them toward me and looking deeply into their eyes. There was something I was looking for, but I couldn't verbalize it if I wanted to. There was something off about the eyes of the fake Cabot, and I was sure I could recognize it if I saw it again. But person after person turned in surprise to me, their eyes a mixture of shock and fear, and none of them felt like the shifter.

A scream rippled through the air near the back of the large lobby, closely followed by a loud bark. I snapped toward the sound and saw several people falling over, knocked over by something barreling through them. That could only be one thing—Dog, and he was on the scent! An old man and his wife hit the deck in a way that made me think they were looking more for a chance to file a lawsuit than anything else, and I ran in their direction.

"I'm coming," I shouted as I headed toward the commotion. A few security guards, still unsure of what exactly was happening, moved to step in front of me. I thought fast and pulled out my small billfold, where I kept the pre-paid credit card Ally slipped me a while ago so I could buy things without her, and flashed it toward them. "FBI! Move!"

One guard looked at the other and shrugged. Both stepped aside in time to clear room for me to leap over the fallen old man and his wife. As I soared over them, the old man and I locked eyes.

"Hey," I said casually as I passed over his face. My feet

hit the floor, and I pounded toward another group of people who seemed like something already tore through the center of them. "Which way did the dog go?" I yelled as I approached them. As one, they pointed down a hallway, and I skidded to a halt so I could head that way.

I was most of the way down the hall and nearing a turn deeper into the maze of conference rooms and offices when a prickling feeling went up my spine and the hair on my arms stood on end. Something was wrong. Something was very wrong. A decade of survival in The Deep tugged at my instincts. I steeled myself as I rounded the corner, not knowing what I was heading into, but knowing it likely involved a fight.

As soon as I turned the corner, two lumbering vampires leapt out at me. One was so slow he missed me and rammed himself into the wall of the narrow hallway. The other caught me by the arm, enough that I went with his momentum and shoved him face-first into a large wooden door. Almost instantaneously as he crashed into the door, I shoved my elbow into his jaw, crushing it between me and the wood. A loud pop came from his mouth, and I knew I broke it.

"A vampire that can't chomp. That's gotta suck."

I rammed my knee into his gut and doubled him over before I turned to face the other one. He was upright and shaking his head from the impact with the wall. I spun into a kick that landed hard on his chest and sent him flying into one of those crappy generic paintings that always seemed to line the halls in places like this. The painting fell and the wooden frame split into pieces. While eyeing the broken shards, I saw my chance to end this fight quickly.

I snatched up one of the sharper pieces and twirled it in my hands as I waited for the vampire to stand and get in the right position. As soon as he was upright while baring his teeth and growling, I thrust forward, pierced him in the heart, and drove him back into the wall. The wood went all the way through his body and nailed him upright against the fading wallpaper.

I turned back to the other vampire, snatched another shard and eyed him closely. He seemed to be reaching for the door handle. I readied myself to charge him before he could get through.

"Going to run, big fella? Good, I have better things to —" I began.

My words stopped in my throat as he opened the door and it slowly swung inward. Before it was halfway open, I saw that I was in a fair amount of trouble. At least a dozen other vampires, all weak ones like these two, were waiting to come through. What they lacked in brains or fighting skill, it seemed they planned to make up for it in sheer numbers.

"Oh, well, that makes it more difficult. Maybe we can do this some other time." I turned to run and stopped again.

More were behind me and blocked the direction of the exit door I was sure the shifter went through. I was looking at a fight with over twenty of these guys. I drew a deep breath and let it out slowly as I looked from one group of vampires to the other while flipping the makeshift stake in my hand.

I can't fight them all. Well, I mean, I could fight them all, but it would take forever, and I don't have the time. I have to find some way to get past them instead. But how?

A sudden burst of light from behind the large group in the hallway grabbed my attention. It swirled in the air, and seconds later, the vampires turned in surprise and anger. A fight had broken out, and something was attacking them from behind. Some*one*. I glimpsed an axe, and my heart jumped. Pip bounded toward me on her tiny legs from the center of the crowd while swinging her axe in large circles and clipping several of the vampires on her way to me.

"Pip! How did you find me?" I exclaimed.

"Followed the trail of destruction. Seems to be your thing." She shrugged.

I shook my head and turned my attention to the open door where the vampires inside had yet to move and were now turning their attention toward Pip.

"Pip? Remember that move I showed you?"

"The one with the spinny-swingy thing and the big boom?"

"Yeah, that one."

"Yes." She nodded enthusiastically.

"Do you think you could run into that room and do that move on these guys while I get through the other ones to keep chasing the shifter?" I encouraged.

"Oh, yeah," she agreed.

"You sure?" I asked.

Pip set the axe down and spat into her hands, rubbed them together, then picked up the weapon. It was taller than she was, and when she rested it on her shoulder, she had to take a step or two backward to stay upright.

"I got this," she confirmed without hesitation.

"Pip, you're awesome. Now go get 'em!" I cheered.

Without missing a beat, Pip let out a massive war cry for such a tiny person and charged into the room. The vampires surrounded her, as expected, and she rushed into the middle of them before spinning in place with the axe. I didn't need to watch what happened next. It would be messy.

I turned and faced the remaining vampires not nursing wounds in the hall. Somewhere beyond them was Dog, and whatever he was chasing. It had to be the shifter. And I would catch it.

CHAPTER THIRTY-SEVEN

I rushed through the vampires at the end of the hall and kicked the one who had regained his footing so he went back down, hard, then continued through the building. Another emergency staircase was behind the only door beyond this point, and I yanked it open before any of the vampires could chase me.

Another bark from above told me I was on the right track, and I raced up the stairs. As I climbed ever higher, more barks alerted me that rather than going for the street level, the shifter must have headed for the roof. Maybe they had a helicopter or something up there.

I finally reached the roof access, burst through the door, and stopped in my tracks in confusion. Dog stood there growling, his teeth bared and his hair on end. The person he was growling at was Ally, who had her palms out toward him as she slowly backed up. Her eyes opened wide with relief when she saw me.

"Sara! Thank God! Dog has gone nuts. Something is wrong with him. Is it possible it's the shifter?" she asked.

The thought briefly ran through my mind that perhaps I had been chasing the shifter all along, but then my brain doubled back to something she said.

Did she call me Sara?

I stalked up to them, went between them, and looked down at Dog. He hadn't moved and was still growling, and it was louder and more pronounced than it had been when I first got on the roof. I knew that growl. I turned to look at Ally, and a white-hot sear of anger brushed over me, and my scalp felt like pins and needles. I hated this.

"Sara, help me." I did, by shoving my fist right into her nose. "What the hell?" she exclaimed as she stumbled backward.

"You aren't Ally," I spat.

"The hell? Sara, look at me! I'm your best friend!" Her eyes were wide and imploring, but she wasn't fooling me.

Dog growled behind me, and I steeled myself. It sure looked like Ally. It sounded like her, too. There was a part of me that wanted to go to her, help her up, and apologize. But my anger overrode that part. I hated that someone would use her face, my best friend's face, to trick me. And that forever, I would have to remember punching her face because they did it.

"You made a mistake, stupid. You called me Sara. Ally doesn't call me Sara. Ally calls me Slick," I told her.

I stepped forward, ready to shove my fist through what looked like my best friend's teeth. Then it morphed, and the skin stretched around bones that moved around like bugs underneath. I struggled to keep looking at it, but maintained my position.

The creature stood. It was taller now, and the clothes

had changed, meaning even the outfit was part of the Shapeshifter's glamour. I recognized those clothes. My heart caught in my throat as the shifter stared at me through eyes I hadn't seen in so long.

"I call you Sara, don't I?" My father's voice came from mere feet in front of me. Part of me wanted to run up and embrace him, to wrap my arms around him and smell his cologne. To forget, for a few precious seconds, that it wasn't real.

"You son of a bitch," I forced out as tears welled up in my eyes. "Don't you *dare* use his image."

The shifter laughed and charged. I fell back a step, fighting with myself to put up my arms to defend against the vision of my father attacking me. It was so surreal, so mind-bending. So *wrong*. Its movements were faster than I anticipated, and my arms seemed too slow to block the fists coming at me.

Each one narrowly missed my face and instead glanced off my cheek or landed hard on my shoulder. I stopped moving backward and thrust forward, smashing my head into its chest, but it barely stepped back at all. Instead, it used the position of my head to land an uppercut that sent me flying backward.

Dog leapt at the shifter, who shrugged him off and smashed his body into the side of an exhaust fan. I was still recovering, so it took the time to turn and land a rib-cracking kick on Dog's side. That snapped me out of my funk and I focused hard on the creature, refusing to let its resemblance to my father confuse me anymore.

I ran hard at the shifter, tackled it in the chest and pushed it back toward the edge of the building. Scaffolding stopped us from going over and down to the street, and heavy hands crushed down into my back, forcing me to let go. As I stood, I saw the body morph again, first ranging back through Ally and Cabot, then a flash of Archie before something far more hideous. Its true form was finally being set free, and I recoiled at the sight of it.

Its skin was like a slick wooden varnish on a rocking chair, brown with long streaks of black, with spotted areas that seemed slicker than others. Pus and ooze drizzled from those areas, and the pus formed into shapes seemingly at random. The secret of its shifting had something to do with that gunk, and it covered the shifter's entire body in a slimy, shiny glaze.

Its head looked like it was a large, upside-down letter "V" with a huge bulbous nose coming out of the center. Wide, deep-set, yellow eyes stared back at me, a small black pupil in each tracking my movements. Its ribcage was visible, and it shifted and moved with the creature's breathing, while long talons on its feet and hands clenched like pincers on a lobster. With what seemed like a waterfall of the yellow ooze suddenly springing from every pore, the body shifted in appearance again, this time settling on a mirror image of me.

I gasped in horror, but the sound cut off as a hand that looked so much like mine reached out, grabbed me by the throat, and tossed me over the edge of the scaffolding. I reached out and snagged a bar right below the level my doppelganger stood on to keep from tumbling to the ground below. My pocket practically vibrated as Splinter shook in fear. I made a note not to reach in that pocket anytime soon unless I wanted a handful of vomit to throw at someone.

"Getting beat up by Daddy was too much for your brain, wasn't it, Slick?" the shifter said in my voice, sending a chill down my spine as my feet dangled high above the ground below. "It's nothing compared to what I'll do next. As soon as I've dealt with you, I'll find Father Dearest while looking like this. Like you. And we'll have such a tearful reunion. So many smiles. Then, right in front of your siblings, I'll rip his heart out of his chest and force them to watch."

High-pitched laughter split the air, and the version of my head above me threw itself back to fully enjoy the experience.

"How do you know all this?" I yelled while trying to kick my feet up to wrap them around something more stable. If I could keep this thing talking, I might find a way to climb up. "How do you know about my family?"

"My boss knows everything about you," the shifter sneered. Then the face morphed again. When it stopped, my grip slipped in surprise, and I nearly tumbled to my death in realization. The face was one I recognized.

"Solon?"

A face looked down on me that I longed to see every time I fought for my life. Solon's eyes looked down, and his mouth curled into a sinister smile.

"Time to die, Slick," a voice I hadn't heard in so long said, and its hand reached down to grasp my fingers.

The rustling in my pocket became more active, and suddenly, a brown blur ran up my chest and jumped onto the face of the shifter wearing Solon's face. Splinter defied his fear of heights and dove into action, trailing a thin line of puke as he did. The combination of a large rat-like thing biting his nose and the stomach-turning smell of Splinter vomit on his chest was enough to distract the shifter for a second.

I took an extreme risk and swung my body like an Olympian on the rings until my momentum brought me back up again. I kicked out hard at the uneven scaffolding, and the shifter lost its balance, then tumbled forward and over the railing. A hand clasped my ankle, and I looked down into Solon's face as I hung by my arms.

"Slick, please help me!" The voice pleaded, sending a chill along my spine.

Splinter ran up the shifter's arm and clawed his hand as he switched from him to me, then settled on my shoulder. He twittered a sound somewhere between relief and anger, and it helped shake me from the instant pang of empathy I felt toward Solon's face below me.

"You failed, dickweed. Ever wondered what it feels like to fly?"

I kicked hard, smashing into the fingers, and the body fell. But instead of falling to the street below, the body hit the railing below us and somehow fell onto the platform. It didn't move. I was pretty sure its back was either broken or severely hurt, and if I tried jumping straight down onto the platform, I might suffer the same fate. I shimmied my way under the platform bar and onto the platform itself.

I stood, then brushed my hands off and flexed them after hanging on so hard.

"Dog, get out of here. I'll meet you at the van," I commanded, and he took off. I drew a deep breath and exhaled slowly while putting my hands on my knees. Splinter nudged into my neck, and I nuzzled him with my cheek.

"Thanks, little guy." I rubbed Splinter's head. "You did really good the—ow!" I yelped as he bit my hand. "What the hell is the matter with you?" I yelled, then saw that he wasn't looking at me.

He was looking behind me. Suddenly, something wrapped around me. It felt like a rope made of electricity, and it bound my hands to my sides. I turned to see Bentham and Thrash, and Bentham using her magic to create a kind of energy rope that captured me.

"Bentham! I'm not the bad guy here. You know that!" I beseeched.

"I'm sorry, Slick. I still have a job to do." The emotion in her voice was hard to decipher.

"Yeah, fuckin' waste her. Let's blow her brains out and get this over with," Thrash interrupted, clearly enjoying the idea of my brain matter being splattered.

Bentham turned to look at him, and I didn't hesitate. I jumped backward blindly off the edge. The rope spell broke, probably due to Bentham's obvious shock. My hands freed themselves in time to grab the lower ledge and pull myself up. I got under the bar on the platform below as Bentham shot out her lasso once more, missing me by inches.

The shifter was gone. I didn't have time to hunt for it again, but I must have underestimated how tough it was. After cursing myself for letting it get away, I kicked a window hard, and the glass exploded inward. I rushed inside and landed in an office with a wide-open door. On the other side of the office door, like a gift from the gods, was an open elevator. I ran to it and slid on the hardwood floor to land inside the elevator before it closed. I jammed the lobby button and waited as the door finally opened on that floor.

When no one rushed inside to grab me, I rolled out, pushed myself against a wall, and looked for the door. A crowd of people was near it, some streaming out in panic, others streaming in with curiosity. Security had given up all hope of controlling it and were instead staring at each other in disbelief.

I threw myself into the crowd and forced my way outside, blending in with the hysterical escapees as I made my way back to Archie and the rest of the group.

CHAPTER THIRTY-EIGHT

"Sir, I believe TSA requirements allow me three ounces of liquids in individual containers as long as they're kept within a zipped quart-size bag. You can measure if you see fit, but please be careful. The water is important."

I was too lost in my fog of funk to fully process what I heard Archie say behind me. We were making our way through Customs so we could head back home, and once again, he'd become locked in a battle of wills against the authorities.

"Sir, this isn't what that rule intended," the agent informed him.

I glanced over my shoulder as I hooked my backpack closed again and saw the agent holding up a zipper bag full of tiny shampoo bottles filled with water and goldfish. His eyes slid to the side to watch their little tails flicking around as they swam up and down the bottles. There was enough room in each for the fish to get to the top, snack on some flakes Archie put in there, turn around, and swim back down.

"Show me the specific regulation that states I am not permitted goldfish," Archie demanded. "If anything, you should commend me for stringently adhering to the regulations. Each fish takes up a considerable volume of water, so I don't have three ounces of fluid in any of those bottles. Don't even attempt to classify them as a gel."

"Sir, I must confiscate these and have them properly disposed of," the agent insisted.

My eyes snapped to Archie, and I saw his face fall. I threw my bag over my shoulder and grabbed Dog, then rushed toward them as fast as I could lug both things.

"Actually, those are for my emotional support dog. They are a critical part of his training." I snatched the bag from the agent.

"They are?" he asked skeptically.

"Yes. And you don't want me to get home and sic the ADA on your insensitive ass, do you?" I asked.

Since that was both rude and illogical, I didn't wait around for him to respond. I stuffed the fish bottles into my backpack, prayed for their safety during the flight, and dragged Dog toward the exit. Behind me, they were herding Archie through the full body scanner.

"Sir, you need to remove the spoon," the agent instructed.

"It's a protective device," Archie insisted.

I'd lost track of Ally and Pip during the shuffle through Customs, but once I dropped into a chair in the waiting area, I caught sight of them. They hurried toward me, and Ally proudly presented me with a large plate of crappy airport tacos. It should have been an utterly delightful gesture, but it didn't cheer me up.

I took a bite and put the plate down. In his half-drugged state, Dog's nose still picked up the scent, and his muzzle shifted and bounced as it sniffed. His head toppled to the side, and his tongue lolled out of his mouth to gather some taco filling. Apparently, a little pain medication went a long way with Dog. I wasn't sure he could chew or swallow in this condition, but he would do his best.

"What's wrong?" Pip asked.

"I feel a little down," I admitted.

"I don't understand. We won! Why would you feel down?" the lizard girl asked. "Look."

She pointed up at the television mounted above us. The audio wasn't loud enough for us to hear it, but we saw the Ambassador and Cabot shaking hands and flashing huge smiles at the camera. The chyron read, "New Day for Peace."

"I know why." Archie finally made his way over to us. "British food sucks."

I appreciated his attempt to cheer me up, but I couldn't quite muster a laugh.

"It's not that. It's...I...I..."

"It's Solon," Ally guessed.

I nodded. "Seeing my old mentor's face, hearing his voice, and watching the man who'd spent almost ten years protecting me try to kill me...it was too much. There was a moment when I was dangling from the roof that I considered the possibility that it was the real Solon attacking me. But I knew that couldn't be true. I saw him die. No faking that."

"You never told me how Solon died," Ally murmured.

"I can't. Not yet. Not now. It's... I can't. I'm sorry," I

added lamely. Ally nodded, but I knew it wasn't the last time I would hear that question. Eventually, I would have to face that terrible moment again, to let it out of the room inside my head that I had barred with everything else I could find that hadn't blocked the memories of my father's face as the Philosophers took me away. I winced at both thoughts. "It was so personal. Hobbes seems to know everything about me, but I know nothing about him. Whatever game Hobbes is playing with me, I don't know how to play it back. But Hobbes is in my head. I know that. Right now, he's winning. In the end, only one of us will walk out of this with our lives."

"We need to let people know," Ally said. "The Philosophers should know the truth."

Archie shook his head. "No one would believe us. We're officially screwed."

Hearing the words seemed to wake something inside me. A new wave of hope and optimism washed over me, and I shook my head at them as I looked each in the eyes. Except for Dog. I simply stared at him briefly and hoped he felt it.

"No. No, we are not," I protested. "We are far from screwed. Look at how far we've come and what we've accomplished. We're so much better off than we used to be."

"I don't know if I'd go straight to us being so much better off than we used to be," Archie said.

"And unless you count these long flights, I don't really think we've come that far," Ally concurred.

I shook my head. "Listen to the two of you. Maybe we haven't progressed in leaps and bounds, but look at what we've done. We know this is personal with me and Hobbes. That's a start. And we've made some important allies along the way." I nodded at the screen and Cabot's smiling face. I knew we'd be able to call on her any time we thought she could help us. "I don't know what Hobbes is really up to, or why. But I know that together, we can kick some ass. No more running. I think it's time to show the world how the outcasts really roll."

EPILOGUE

The suit was unwieldy and constricting, but necessary. Without it, the room Hobbes was about to step into would be unbearable. That was the point. To be unbearable. The vacuum-like structure at the bottom sucked all the moisture out of the air, bit by bit, hour by hour, until it was as dry as brittle, burned paper.

Like a colossal dehumidifier, this contraption was designed solely for one purpose—to suck the wet from anything near it. The suit, as gangly as it was, kept Hobbes safe from it by refilling itself with clean, wet air from a tank. Hobbes smiled through the wide visor on the front and walked inside.

The defeated face of the shifter, no longer capable of making itself look like anyone else since all its oozy, gunky moisture had long since evaporated, barely moved when Hobbes came in. It wouldn't be long now before the body simply gave up and died. Maybe he needed to turn the intensity down a tad, if for no other reason than to make the pain last a little longer.

"Hello," Hobbes said in a pleasant voice that mocked the pain he was putting the shifter through. The glee of hurting this creature was almost euphoric.

"Please, let me die. I did what you asked."

"Oh, but you didn't, did you?" Hobbes said in a voice not unlike a kindergarten teacher speaking to a troublesome boy. That's what the shifter was, anyway. A troublesome boy. But rather than a dunce hat, or time out, he was being dried to death. "You failed. Miserably. Not only is Sara Slick still alive, but she saw you for what you really were, and you gave up far too much information, which gave her a clue about who I really am." Hobbes made a tooth-sucking sound and contemplated what to do next. "I really cannot allow such catastrophic failure, you know. Bad for my image."

"I didn't give you up. I gave her nothing," the shifter whined.

"Slick is clever, and she will figure it out given enough time. And now, she has more time, doesn't she? She will come for me if she figures it out. You and I both know this. So, yes, you failed me. You failed me miserably."

"What should we do now, boss?" came a voice from outside the chamber. Hobbes turned to look at its owner. The loyal minion asking for instructions, and willing to lay down his life for his boss. Hobbes was sure it would come to that, if only because he was so damned tiresome. He asked for instruction too often. Servants needed to have more ambition.

But he had a point. What to do now that Sara Slick would come directly for Hobbes? He reached into the control panel and ticked the level down a notch. The euphoric feeling filled Hobbes again. The shifter would live a little longer in immense pain.

Hobbes liked that.

No more outsourcing. No more minions. Even through the massive gloves Hobbes now wore, his hands were getting dirty. Gloriously, disgustingly dirty.

"Nothing," Hobbes replied in a distant voice. "Let her come. I will kill her myself."

The End

Look for Sara's return in book four, *Invade The Heights*, coming soon to Amazon and Kindle Unlimited.

Hey gang!

Lee here. Huge huge HUGE thanks for reading *Fight the Peace*.

I'm a big fan of small-town hero stories, but for this one we wanted to change it up by throwing Slick into a Mission Impossible-styled adventure, complete with face swaps and aerial stunts and a trip across the pond.

Which, quite frankly, was pretty refreshing to work on while self-isolating.

I don't know about you, but I love to travel (and Chris is downright obsessed with it). And while not-traveling for fun isn't that big of a burden, all things considered, it's been weird spending this spring and summer at home or without out of town friends coming to visit during Coronavirus. A break with the normal by not breaking normal, if that makes sense.

But that's the beauty of books, right? Our heroes can go and do and see what we can't, our fictional friends are always in reach, and adventure is only a click away.

So whatever your Covid situation is right now (even if it is long, long gone), I hope you're finding the kind of escape you need, and I hope that we've helped in some small way with our fiction (and if we did, ahem, you could let us know on Amazon and over at the Facebook page).

Alright, time to escape back into my writing.

Catch you later!

Lee Barbant

PS: Want to hear more from us? Sign up for our newsletter and also receive a FREE copy of *The Devil's Due,* our fast and fun thriller:

https://www.subscribepage.com/chris_and_lee

<u>Sign up</u> for Chris and Lee's newsletter for updates, new releases, and promotions. When you join the community, you'll get a FREE copy of their fast, fun thriller, *The Devil's Due:* https://www.subscribepage.com/chris_and_lee

Want more snarky heroines? Well, Chris and Lee also have an urban fantasy series about the mythic gods return to earth in their series with ST Branton, *Forgotten Gods*. The tagline is: *The gods are real, and they're assholes.* And it couldn't be closer to the truth. This series is fun, fast, exciting, and a little irreverent.

Vampires, werewolves, and all manner of monstrous creatures serve the unknown powers of old, but the story centers on the humans who make the heroic choice to fight them. Join Vic and her crew as they attempt to save earth from the gods who want it back. You won't forget, Forgotten Gods.

Oh, and… it is an 8 book omnibus almost always on sale for silly cheap!

While you're at it, we really thing you should try the new and improved *Steel City Heroes*:

A mad scientist fighting the laws of man and nature.

A demon-monster of mythical proportions.

A corporate conspiracy that goes back more than a century.

The Steel City is in desperate need of a hero.

Happy Reading!!

www.ingramcontent.com/pod-product-compliance
Lightning Source LLC
Chambersburg PA
CBHW050234110726
47898CB00007B/2140